This novella was written within twenty-four hours in aid of Shelter Scotland.

Shelter Scotland's aim is as follows:

"We exist to defend the right to a safe home and fight the devastating impact the housing emergency has on people and society.

We do this with campaigns, advice and support—and we never give up.

We believe that home is everything."

All royalties earned from the sales of this novella are donated to Shelter Scotland via Work For Good.

NO PLACE THAT'S HOME

A novella written within 24 hours in aid of Shelter Scotland

Written by Scott G.G. Crowden

10AM 30th June – 8AM 1st July 2024

This is a work of fiction. Names, characters, places and incidents either are the product of the author's imagination or are used fictitiously. Any resemblance to actual persons, living or dead, events, or locales is entirely coincidental.

Copyright © 2024 by Scott G.G. Crowden

All rights reserved. No part of this book may be reproduced or used in any manner without written permission of the copyright owner except for the use of quotations in a book review. For more information, contact scottcrowdenauthor02@gmail.com

First paperback edition August 2024

Book cover design by Carin from GetCovers

ISBN: 9798333117793

@scottcrowdenauthor on Facebook & Instagram

NO PLACE THAT'S HOME

CHAPTER ONE
Lynda, Darryl, Ellie & Jack

It's been two months since Lynda was fired from her job. She worked in a manufacturing company for thirteen years—a fourth of her entire life—and yet due to budget cuts she was thrown to the curb before she could even process it.

There were many *sorry's* and *our greatest apologies*, but none of it made Lynda feel any better because she was still without a job. Saying sorry doesn't pay the bills.

At first, it struck her as a tragedy; she spent hours each day moping, sobbing for minutes at a time while her three children asked her what's wrong. It brought her down into a hole that had been dug under her home for years, right under her nose. She should have seen it coming, really. It started with a slight pay cut, then reduced hours, and then laid off.

She applied for work—a new, fresh job to clear her mind. But even with her decade of experience, the demand for jobs is tight and ever-increasing. She managed to land a couple of interviews, but with tens of other interviewees, the chosen few were young, more prospective and more naïve than she is. After her sacking, she began to ask more cautious, or more *real* questions, but the interviewers didn't like it.

So two months on, she's still without a job, and with three children living under her roof, the expenses are rising and her bank account is dwindling. The AC unit has broken and, to the dismay of all, she's had to temporarily cut off the internet. The first few days were the worst: her middle child, Ellie, began to act like the world had begun to crumble around her.

And in a way, she was right.

It occurs to Lynda that she's going to have to make some drastic decisions sooner rather than later. She could apply for benefits, but with her skilled expertise in her arsenal, she knows that she is more than capable of securing a job. A working woman, she doesn't think she could take on benefits, for there's still so much work out there for her to do.

The decisions she has to make worsen day by day, and even her children notice the freedoms in their life escape them. At first it was the internet, and then it was the gas, the heating, and showers that lasted more than two minutes. Now one minute.

Lynda loves to cook meals for her children, but she doesn't like cooking with cheap, off-brand ingredients. She wants her children to eat the best of the best, to be the best of the best, but without money it just isn't possible. Her lifestyle has changed to fit this newfound poverty. Instead of her weekly shop on Mondays at 7AM in the supermarket, she tends to visit the supermarket around 8PM, where the reduced yellow sticker items are put out.

There are now less family trips out. No more *Burger King*, no more fun parks, no more arcade nights, no more movie nights. If her kids are lucky, they'd be treated to a movie haul from the one pound section in the supermarket. Darryl, her eldest, is reminded of his upbringing as a young child, when online on-demand movie streaming was less common.

While her children find themselves lost in the many worlds inside the TV, in her bedroom, Lynda struggles with the real world, filing through papers and invoices, rent notices and rent increases, denials and rejections from companies and firms, dentists and doctors notes from months ago. Her heart has slowed down to a pace where it barely beats at all. Everything has slowed down into a deep depression.

When the landlord comes to visit, she asks for him to come only when the kids are at school, so as to not alarm them of their impending eviction. After six months of unpaid rent, he stops abiding by her requests, and visits whenever he feels like it.

"Mum, are we going to be kicked out of the house?" Jack, her youngest child of three years, asks her after the landlord's last visit. His eyes seem utterly conscious and thinking.

At first, she isn't sure how to respond. It's hard with the little ones—you never know exactly how much they'll understand, or how much they'll retain. Sugarcoating sometimes just confuses them and simplifying often comes across as too blunt.

"Yes, I think so," she says with a smile, "but it's nothing to worry about—we'll be staying with Auntie Lydia for a while, and she's got a nice house. You'll like it. But we'll only be staying there for a while, mind you. Just think of it as a holiday."

"We're going on holiday?"

Lynda's lips strain as they smile. "Yeah, we are. Run along and tell your brother and sister."

Two weeks later, Lynda moves into her sister Lydia's house, carrying with her, her three children and a van-full of luggage to boot. Ellie and Jack are at first over the moon, the prospect of travelling somewhere at the other side of the country and living in a new house with internet and *PlayStation* and *YouTube* truly an exciting one. Darryl, being nineteen years old, knows better though. He understands the sadness of it all, and of how he's been forced to cut ties with his friends back home, to distance himself from them, miles apart.

Worst yet is that Darryl was in part time work at a hotel, working as a waiter and earning some extra cash to help fund his university tuition for the coming year. Now, with his mother's sacking, he, too, has been forced out of his job.

He does his best to ride along with the act that Lynda puts on for the kids, but sometimes he can't help but fill the room with pessimism, groaning and complaining about the situation that they find themselves in. The conversations between mother and son are now rarely without an argument or debacle that ends in slammed doors and muted shouts from across the house.

Lydia's house is smaller than Lynda's. She hasn't visited her sister in years, so this fact had escaped her, but as she begins to unpack her family's belongings, it truly occurs to her just how densely packed her life will become.

A three bedroom bungalow, Lynda's entire side of the family are forced into one single room, one spring bed, reserved for the two youngest, a sleeping bag for Darryl and after putting her children to sleep, Lynda creeps into the living room and rests herself upon the sofa, sleeping through many restless, noisy nights and waking at the crack of dawn. Her back soon begins to ache, her neck feels twisted, crooked as her body reaches out longer than the sofa itself. She is often awoken by the roar of cars outside or from the gulls that squawk the rising of the sun into being. Her bright blue eyes are soon carried by bags.

The house is chaotic. Lydia herself has two children, both in primary school, and a dog, Chuck, that liked attention and liked eating all of the food. Lydia doesn't like the way that her sister treats the dog—as if he's less important than they are—and there are many awkward and intense arguments about it. Once, Darryl overhears his aunt ranting about his mother and of how she could evict the lot of them at any moment. When he decides to tell his mother about it, all hell soon breaks loose.

It isn't just the parents, either; the children find themselves entangled in a wicked web of confrontation, too. Lydia's kids liked having the liberty of having the gaming console to themselves and of being able to play hide and seek with just the two of them. But now there's two other children hogging the controller, always asking to join and crying whenever they're told no. And the older one? The dark, harsh eyes resting underneath his fringe scares them, and sometimes they don't feel safe in their own home.

Weeks pass without much progress. Lynda sits waiting for any source of hope from the tens of companies that she applied to, from the council and from the many advisors that she contacts in search of aid. Darryl finds some new friends but Lydia says they're the wrong crowd, indulging in drugs on the regular, and Ellie and Jack go weeks without an education, the awe of the temporary summer holidays soon wearing off.

But there's nothing they can do—not that Lynda knows of, anyway. Her husband died in a car crash only two weeks after Jack's birth, and her parents died of old age. She has a few relatives, but most of them live abroad. Lydia is her only hope, but even she seems to be turning against her, her own home beginning to feel like another's.

By all means, Lynda and her family are well and truly *homeless.*

One night after a particularly tense dinner, Lynda sits alone with Ellie, who stares at her with wet eyes, her childlike innocence pierced by her mother's despair. As if she was the parent in the relationship, she grabs her mother's arm. Lynda manages to smile—a genuine one, at that—until Ellie speaks.

"When are we going home?" She asks.

It has been about a month since they moved out, and yet not once have her children asked her this question. She knew it was coming at some point, and she dreaded it. There's no answer because even she doesn't know. There's surely some sort of salvation out there, but then where is it?

As her quivering lips move, so do the waterworks.

"Home's gone, sweetie," she says, tearing up, "we're not going back anytime soon."

CHAPTER TWO
Craig & Annie

It's a cold and wet night in Aberdeen, which is quite usual. Down by Beach Boulevard, a large throng of vehicles for the biweekly car show rev their engines. Even from his window, Craig can hear each and every car, and of the sounds that seem to him like that of an apocalyptic wasteland, of the end of the world. Some of the cars are followed by police vehicles, while others speed onto the giant grass patch and swirl around and around, leaving donuts.

Craig used to be into modifying his car, but when little Annie was born, he had to put that hobby to the side for a while. He's never really gotten back to it, and now, watching these cars rev, honk their horns and generally just ooze obnoxiousness, he doesn't think he'll ever find the love for it again. Some of the cars impress him, but when you've got a little girl trying to sleep in the room next to you, it would be better if they just shut up.

"Oh, jeez," Craig sighs, knowing that Annie's going to wake up, "thanks for that."

He closes the window shut and makes sure that it's properly closed. If it's not properly closed, the cars will still sound like they're zooming right past the flat. There's that, and the constant fear of a crash. A car has crashed right outside of his flat four times in the past month. Most people blame the council for the road, but he blames the drivers.

It's 10PM and he's still wide awake, so he decides to cook something. He's already had dinner, but that was aligning with Annie's dinner time, which is around 4PM. Before she was born, he usually ate dinner around 9PM. A far cry from what he was, you'd think that he was happy with his new lifestyle, but frankly eating dinner that early still feels wrong.

"OK, what's in store tonight?" He says to himself, opening up the fridge as if he has no idea what's inside. It's mostly full of beer and various vegetables that are useless without something to add to them, to mix them in with. Craig doesn't like salads.

That's something that both he and Annie agree on. Green stuff is nasty.

There's nothing in the fridge that appetises him, so he checks the freezer instead. There, he finds a ready meal for two, lasagne. It takes forty-five minutes to cook, which is about as long as he can go before he starves, so he reluctantly lugs it in the oven.

Relaxing with his arms resting behind his head, he mindlessly watches some reality television, where a dozen celebrities are living in the jungle in Australia, all outside of the comfort of their own home and forced to live amongst the wilderness. Homelessness is entertaining when it's people you recognise, like D-list celebrities. It's fun for them to pretend to be stranded, to be forced to fend for themselves and fight for food. It's fun for Craig, too, as he sees his favourite *Corrie* star eat a plateful of horse testicles.

Of course, he's seen all of the rumours online that the celebrities aren't actually left alone — that they're fed off-camera, supplied with makeup and handed their mobile phones.

While waiting for the lasagne to cook, he nibbles on tortilla chips, and makes his way through about half of a packet before he decides to stop. He craves tzatziki, and he *does* have some in the fridge, but he can't be bothered standing up to get it.

More for later, he thinks, trying to phase out his laziness.

In the corner of his eye, he sees Annie standing between the gap in her bedroom door, watching him and debating whether or not she should enter the living room. The loud roar of car engines outside makes her flinch occasionally, as though bombs are going off outside. She's making enough noise so that Craig can blatantly hear her, but he acts the fool, aloof as he's immersed in the TV, chewing on his chips.

"Dad...?" She whispers. Craig pretends not to hear her in hopes that she'll simply go back to sleep. But as the door creeps fully open, he has no choice.

"What are you doing up at this time?" He asks, half-scolding and half-worried, "It's long past your bedtime. Are all of those cars waking you up again?"

Annie nods, her stuffed penguin held tight in her arms.

"Ach, you can come through here and sit with me for a wee while. Not too long though—you've still got school tomorrow morning. You've practised your times tables, haven't you, sweetheart?"

A spring in her step, Annie leaps onto the seat across from the sofa. "Yeah. I know them all off by heart now, Dad."

"What's seven times eight?"

"Fifty-six, silly."

"Wow, you've really gotten good, you clever thing," Craig chuckles, "You're faster than I am, and I'm about five times your age."

"You're stupid, Dad."

"Hey now! Enough of that or you'll be going right back to sleep."

The room is full of laughter. Craig feels a little humiliated but it's his own daughter, so he assures himself that there's nothing to be ashamed of. If your child is smarter than you, then it still counts because they came *from* you, right? If they're smart, then you must be, too.

The two sit in silence for a while, Craig engrossed in the nothingness of reality TV and Annie lost in the confusing complex of times tables. She's trying to learn the eleven and twelve times tables, not because she has to but because she wants to impress her teacher—some kids call her a teacher's pet, but it doesn't bother her much.

The flat is small, but it's theirs. A mould of Craig's slightly stubby figure has been made into the couch, while the chair suits no one better than Annie. Some of the walls, painted grey, have colourful scribbles on them from when Annie was younger, but Craig likes them as this is as much of her flat as his. Of course, only *he* pays the rent.

It's a little messy, but it's a lived-in messy. Craig does his best to clean but sometimes the plate in the sink can stay there, and the cluster of cornflake crumbs that fell to the ground isn't going to do anyone any harm if it stays there for another day or two. The kitchen counter is barely visible underneath a wealth of Annie's toys, but there's no point in putting them away when she's going to play with them tomorrow anyways.

If the flat was empty, it wouldn't really feel like a home at all.

The ringing of Craig's phone, which he left in his jacket pocket, is muted by the loud roar of car and motorbike engines. Annie can sense the vibration and looks around at the dimmed room for the source, but thinks very little of it. By now, she can smell the gentle ooze of the lasagne come out of the oven.

The phone rings and rings, but it isn't until an advert break that Craig hears it. At first he groans, the prospect of having to stand to pick it up an unwelcome one. But when it's still ringing minutes later, he figures it must be important, and so he leaps out of the sofa and grabs it from his hooked coat.

"Hello? Who is this?" He asks, slightly miffed.

Annie watches her father's face under close examination. She's learned in her short period with a full consciousness that phone calls, when unexpected, often mean ill. This seems to be no different, and she fears who is calling her father. His face turns from an inquisitive scowl to exasperated in shock, to furrowed in determination and grit. He looks at Annie briefly which scares her, as if she's involved in this somehow. She rises to her feet as her father wraps his coat around his arms and grabs his car keys.

When he hangs up, he calls her. "Come on, Annie, put your shoes on. Don't worry about getting dressed, you can stay in your pyjamas. Just put your shoes on quickly, please."

While in the car, Craig is driving about as fast as the racers at the car show earlier. His eyes are dead-set on the road, as if he has a mission to complete. Annie holds onto snowy, her stuffed penguin, as if he will save her from a potential crash. She wants to ask her father what happened and why he's in such a rush, but she can't get the words out. Intense situations like this scare her. She doesn't know what's going on. How she should feel.

When Craig glances to look at her, he realises this.

"Your uncle's been in a car accident," he says in a tone as calm as he can be, "we're just going over to the hospital to check on him. The nurse said it was very bad."

Annie's eyes widen. She feels like she wants to cry but doesn't know how to.

Uncle Rab is basically a second father to her. Mum died when she was young, so whenever Dad was unable to look after her when he was working overtime or had some event to go to, uncle Rab would always take care of her instead. He's quite a bit older than Dad, so Annie was never sure how the two of them could be brothers.

Rab is always up and at 'em'. He taught Annie how to ride her bike, even when Craig said she was too young for it. He's also taught her how to scavenge for mushrooms, how to tell apart poisonous from harmless ones, and how to cut them up and cook them. Whenever Craig's gone for a whole weekend, Rab takes her camping. She loves camping.

But she knows about death, and of how people die from car crashes. Her little heart begins to tense up, to cry because her eyes can't. She doesn't say anything for the rest of the drive.

The two of them are out of the car only seconds after arriving at the car park. Craig is in an awful rush, which seems to only confirm Annie's worries. She holds on tight to his hand as he takes her on a turbulent ride through the reception and into A&E.

The doctors let them straight through to the ward, which Annie, even in her young age, realises is strange, and is mostly a bad omen. The last time she was here, when she grazed her arm against the ground, leaving a big, grazed stroke of blood, she had to wait for hours.

Hiding behind her father, she enters the room in which Rab is being held. Inside, it's chaotic as it is outside. Doctors and nurses race back and forth, shouting words that Annie doesn't understand to one another. One nurse stops to debrief Craig on his brother's current status. The frown on her face instils impossible levels of terror into her.

"His accident was fatal," the nurse says, "we're trying our best here, but I'm afraid it isn't looking too good. You can speak to him if you wish—he's still conscious."

Craig thanks the nurse and pushes her aside. For a moment it's like Annie doesn't even exist; Craig doesn't look back to check if she's there, or to check if she's OK. All he cares for is his dying brother, laid out upon a surgical table. The nurses said they're doing what they can, but Annie can't see anyone trying to help him. He must be too far gone.

"Rab, Rab, stay with me." Craig says, grabbing his brother's hand.

Annie stands next to her father, but is too small to see exactly what Rab, in his dying state, looks like. She's fine with that. All she wants is to hear his voice.

"Is that you, Craig boy?" Rab says. His voice sounds like it's in the other room.

"Yeah, it's me. Annie's here too."

"Annie?" Rab laughs. "You're a magic wee girl. But Craig, you should probably get her out of here—you don't want her to see me…not like this…especially if…"

Craig looks back and forth between his brother and his daughter. Weirdly enough, Annie's face makes him feel worse than Rab's does. He's still got a smile on his face—he always does—and makes light of the situation. Craig looks to the nurses for their affirmation.

"Annie, you should do as your uncle says. The nurse here will take you to the waiting room and I'll come meet you soon. I shouldn't be long." When he says the latter sentence, his face seems to sap of all energy, as if he said something that his mind didn't pick up on.

Annie does as told and is escorted out by a kind, warm nurse. She hugs the nurse's legs as she walks, then strides to the waiting room. The nurse wraps her arm around Annie's back, the motherly embrace that Annie has never felt.

It feels like hours until Craig comes back. Annie expects the worst and it's immediately confirmed the moment that he walks through the double doors. The warm nurse accompanies him, and a part of Annie hopes that she comes home with them.

Craig crouches down to meet Annie's level, but she speaks before he does.

"Uncle Rab is dead, isn't he?"

Craig's mouth thins. His dry eyes suddenly begin to erupt, stream down with floods of tears that have been repressed all night. Seeing her Dad cry like this makes Annie cry too, and the two of them embrace, huddled together in each of their misery. The nurse joins in too, and while Annie can't see her, she imagines that she must be in tears, too.

On the ride back home, Craig explains what happened to Rab. He was driving home from work at the oil and gas company that he works for when a car in front of him abruptly stopped, causing Rab to crash into him. This was only a small graze, but it created a domino effect, where another car turning the corner at the junction also crashed into him. This other car, which was a speeding, modified car from the beachside car show, is what killed him.

You're a magic wee girl. Rab's last words spoken to her rest in her mind. They torment her, upset her, but more than anything remind her of how much she loved him. Even in his last moments, he looked down upon her with a smile on his face.

"My brother's gone," Craig says, speaking to no one in particular, "that's almost everyone now. Mum, Dad, Rab, Christine. Even Aunt Morna. Who the hell am I buying Christmas presents for this year? Annie's gonna get spoiled."

It's clear to Annie that he's fighting back tears, but he fights well. She's never seen her Dad cry before. Tonight was the first time and her heart hopes that it's the last.

But just as things have calmed down, Craig's face lights up as he turns into the street where their flat is located. There's some sort of commotion, and a dozen people are all lined up on the street, looking up towards a pillar of smoke that rises into the sky. Craig's distraught, panicked, defeated face tells Annie everything she needs to know.

Craig speeds up, forcing the bystanders to leap out of the way, and drifts towards his block of flats. Parking on the pavement, he wastes no time in exiting the car. Annie struggles to open the car door but eventually manages to jump out and follow her dad.

When she catches up, she sees her Dad talking with an elderly neighbour, who is pointing up towards their block of flats and to the flames that engulf it.

The neighbour says, "that's your flat, isn't it, Craig?"

CHAPTER THREE
Todd

Todd, in his eighty-three years of living, has resided in the same house. He was delivered here by his father, who had all of the skills of a housewife, and has since inherited it. His father died when he was sixteen, and his mother lived until the exact day of his fifty-sixth birthday. Now, the house is all in his name.

Todd's days pass leisurely. He always feared living in a retirement home or contracting some illness or disease that would mentally impair him, but life has, to some extent, been kind to him. He can still live in his home, and doesn't have to take any pills, apart from painkillers, but everyone's on painkillers, aren't they?

He's still social and talks his mind to some of his neighbours, day-in, day-out. On weekends he tends to go for lunch or dinner with some of his peers, if he's feeling fancy. He's started going to bingo, too, although he can't be bothered actually playing it.

Everything's going well for him, except for his physical impairment.

Todd has been chair bound for ten years now. The day of his accident was his last day of work—it wasn't supposed to be, of course, but that's how it ended up.

He worked with heavy machinery in a factory, and worked nine hours a day, six days a week. His only break would be for church on Sundays. It didn't bother him, though, as he loved to work, and especially into his early seventies, it would get him moving. For years he had to endure his coworker's advice to retire, but he wouldn't have any of it. He still maintained a higher output than they did, even when he was thirty years older than most.

But in the end, their caution was validated when the accident happened. While working with a crushing machine, Todd was crushing pieces of rubbish to be burned and recycled, but the pile was overloaded. It was a stupid manoeuvre to kick the trash further inside, especially with his frail legs, but he did so in complacency.

When he thrust his leg into the machine, his leg cramped, and as he yelled out and recoiled from the pain, his back accidentally brushed against the ON button.

The rest is history. The pain that he felt in those next few moments were immeasurable.

A week later, he was discharged from the hospital, and with an amputated leg. He walked on crutches for the first year, but after a while he felt his strength seeping from his body, and so he resorted to riding himself around in a wheelchair. He hated it at first, and would scowl at anyone that complimented his decision or commended him. He's a working man, and to a working man there's nothing worse than being rendered immobile.

Now and then, he'll climb out of his wheelchair and walk on his crutches, but each time he does so he feels weaker than the last. Sometimes he finds difficulty in holding himself upright, and his other leg forgets how to walk. After many accidents both in the house and out and about, he decides one day to remain in the chair for the rest of his life.

Everything's different now. His house is two-storey, which means that whenever he heads upstairs to bed or to use the bathroom, he has to climb the stairs. He installed a stairlift three years ago, but even that is a struggle to operate sometimes.

The doorways are too small for the wheelchair to fit through. The closet is even worse. Certain drawers in the kitchen are jammed so far into the corner that he needs to either climb out of his wheelchair and crawl or pull out the table from the kitchen entirely to gain access to them. He struggles to reach the high shelves of the top row of the fridge so now they all sit empty with nothing in them.

The house was built by his great grandfather over a hundred years ago, and so it doesn't accommodate his needs. Back then no one in the family was in a wheelchair, nor did anyone ever think that someone would be, Architecture back then was much different, too, where corridors and stairs tended to be much narrower, tight for space but efficiently built.

But now look at it. It's more of a sick joke. His wheelchair is dented in many places, mainly at the front, from the sheer amount of times that he's crashed into the wall.

It might have been his home once, but it sure as hell doesn't feel like his anymore.

He would renovate it if he could, but deconstructing and reconstructing an entire house isn't a cheap endeavour. He's saved up and paid for the stairlift and a ramp to replace the stairs leading up to the house, but that's all he's managed to pay for.

At such an old age, he now wonders whether or not there's any point in saving up to renovate the house to his needs. So instead, he spends his pension money on those expensive lunches, on rich, aged wine and to leave in his will to his grandson, Pete.

This isn't to say that he neglects the house, though. He still keeps care of it, but he feels more like an outside cleaner than anything else. It's common for him to find something hidden far back in a cupboard or in the closet that he forgot about completely. He once ventured into the attic, which was more hassle than anything else he's endured in the past ten years. He needed Pete's assistance, but even then it was a difficult task.

Pete visits once a week, but ever since he secured a new job and became a father, he's had less opportunities to help his old man out. Todd also notices that he doesn't seem to enjoy coming over much anymore, mostly because Todd always has some nagging request for him.

What really got an argument going was discussion about the house itself. While Pete is indebted to his grandfather for he intends to leave a great deal of wealth in his will, Todd is also insistent that he leave the house to him, too, but Pete isn't sure of it. If Todd leaves the house to Pete, he expects him to *live* in it, to continue the family tradition, but Pete's wife doesn't want to live in the city. She wants to live out in the country, set up their own little farm and live quietly, away from the hustle and bustle.

"This is *your* house, son," Todd always says to him, "you just don't have it yet."

"I told you, grandad, I don't need it," Pete stresses, having repeated this conversation over and over again, "I know we've had it for decades, but I'd probably just rent it out."

"No! You cannae do that. Our family lives in this house. Always."

This argument can go on for hours. It often resorts to Pete guilt tripping his grandfather, speaking of all he does for him and how he has no reason to feel tied to his house. Most of the time, Todd caves in and apologies, but Pete knows full well that the same thing is going to happen next time he visits. Once, he contacted a doctor to see if Todd had contracted dementia.

Of course, he doesn't have dementia. He's just immovable and stubborn. Pete felt terrible saying it to him, accusing his own grandfather of having such a disastrous condition.

Todd always feels depressed whenever Pete leaves. He accepts, little by little, that Pete is not going to stay in the house when he eventually passes. He doesn't want to accept it, but he has to. Perhaps he'll only accept it in death, in the afterlife.

Until then, the house will remain without a tenant. Todd might sleep inside, but he's not the tenant, *not really*. A house only becomes a home when someone lives in it, makes it their own, and becomes the hub for that person's life. Todd's house was that at some point, but now it's just a shadow of his former self, belonging to someone who died years ago.

    He's homeless in a house that he's lived in all his life. It acts against him, doesn't suit his needs and refuses to become his grandson's aegis. It might be his family's, but his family are all gone, or at least those who lived in it. The house is now only his shelter, not his place of warmth, of security, of belonging. He's a lone wanderer, travelling from room to room in his wheelchair. Apart from the armchair positioned in front of the TV, nothing feels his.

    But he's not going to move—he knows this. This isn't *his* home anymore, but he'll continue to sleep and reside here until he dies. The house will be fit for someone else.

CHAPTER FOUR
Craig & Annie

An over cooked tray of lasagne is enough to set an entire block of flats on fire. That's a fact, but it's one that Craig doesn't want to admit.

Sitting on the curb outside of the apartment block, Annie's nose is buried in her father's chest, hugging him tightly as to shield herself from the world. The fire engines are still lined up outside of the building, a few brave firefighters extinguishing the flames.

Word is that it's only their flat that has burned down. The corridor connecting some of the flats has been badly marred, too, and is in a dire state of repair, but at least no one was living there. Still, various tenants living in the building are now put on the street, cursing and complaining about Craig and of how inconsiderate he could be. Leaving lasagne in the oven for four hours? How did he not remember to turn it off?

Whenever they start to get on his nerves, Craig bluntly says, "I had to go to the hospital to see my brother. He just died."

This does one of two things; the tenant will suddenly switch, their scowls becoming frowns and their words of scorn becoming those of sorrow. The others show their truest wicked sides, ranting on and on and refusing to back down, saying that it doesn't matter what happened. He should've known better than to leave the oven on.

The worst part of it all is that they're not wrong.

The two sit in silence until the firefighters come back down. The flames dying down incite a small level of hope into both father and daughter, but Craig is smart enough to know that anything that could possibly have been salvaged won't be enough. The house will likely be uninhabitable. He strokes Annie's head to console her. Still snuggled tight, she refuses to let go of her grip on her stuffed penguin. It's the only thing she might have left.

When the firefighters have descended the building, most of the tenants rush towards them and ask if they're OK to go back inside, and if they should worry about the smoke and if they should wear masks or if they'll be in trouble if they have asthma or if the fire spread anywhere else in the building or if it's really hot inside or if they're at any risk. Everyone seems to have a question except for Craig and Annie themselves.

One firefighter approaches the two of them, and pauses before speaking. "I'm afraid most of your flat has been burnt to a crisp. It's quite bad, I'm afraid to say. There might be some things that are still intact, but you shouldn't go back in until you're given the say-so as it might not be safe for you at the moment. The fire has made certain parts of the roof fall down, and the ground itself seems unstable. It'll take a long time to repair."

Craig looks up, his eyes dead. "Thanks for letting me know."

"Oh, and I managed to collect this from the rubble. I thought you should have it, little one," he says, passing a small chocolate sweet over to Annie. She seems hesitant to take it from him, as though her mouth will light on fire the moment that she takes a bite, but she does so anyway, as to not be rude.

"Thank you, mister."

Accepting utter and total defeat, Craig stands up and hoists Annie over his shoulders as he gets the feeling that she won't want to walk at the moment. He queries various firefighters and policemen that show up and asks them what he should do and who he should contact. He's told many things, and it's a lot to take in at once, but he notes all of it down on his mobile phone, which only has thirteen percent battery. The policeman advises that he stay with a relative or find a cheap hotel for the night, and then he can begin to sort things out the next day.

After Rab's death, he can't stay with any of his relatives as he isn't close to any of them, both socially and in terms of physical distance. Annie's all he's got.

In what feels like a drive of shame, he finds the nearest hotel and books it for the night. He debates booking it for a few more nights, but the concept alone scares him—he doesn't want to accept that he'll have nowhere to live after tonight.

Neither he nor Annie sleep much that night. He's borrowed a phone charger from the receptionist downstairs after telling her his story, but he needs to return it to her the next morning. Apart from his car, his wallet in his pocket and the clothes he's wearing, he's lost close to everything. The same goes for Annie—the few items that she's come to garner an attraction to over her short lifetime have all burnt to a crisp.

Her first fondest memories are all gone now.

Twelve hours later, Craig is trying to assuage the damages. He's trying to cover them up to Annie, although he knows full well that she's not stupid anymore. She's growing up fast, and she's likely as aware of the situation as he is. It is needless to say that she hasn't gone to school this morning, nor will she for the foreseeable future.

In her favourite fast food joint, Craig has spoiled her. He's bought her a kids meal, but with extra fries, which is her favourite part of the meal. The joint has a ball pit, and he's booked it for an entire hour just for her — a little greedy, perhaps, but he wants to get her mind off of all of what occurred last night. And seeing her jumping around, diving into the ball pit makes him feel a little better, too, although he knows there's nothing to be happy about.

It's hard for him to watch Annie having fun when he's constantly on the phone, however, first with the police and then with the council and then with the housing agency.

The housing agency call really hurts him. The woman on the phone's tone is all cheery and considerate, which bodes well, but when they get down to the nitty gritty of it, she tells him that without home insurance, there's not much he can do. His landlord isn't happy with what happened — and understandably — and tells him that the repairs will come all from Craig's pocket, not his. Unless he can sort it out soon, he'll be out of a contract and will have nowhere to stay even after the repairs are complete.

He knows it's going to be a staggering amount, but he then asks for a quote from a fire repair firm for how much the repairs would cost him. The total amount, with all things considered, is even larger and more daunting than he had previously imagined.

His bank account isn't exactly booming, and his job's salary is about average. He has the time to make a decision, but he sees no feasible way that he'll be able to pay for the repairs anytime soon. It seems like he's going to be forced out of the home. He rests his forehead in his hands and mutes his screams through a closed mouth.

"Look, this is a terrible situation you've found yourself in," says his landlord, "but at the end of the day, you're liable for what happened. You don't have insurance and I sure as hell can't pay for all of that. I would be willing to help you out a little, but it's not going to be nearly enough to pay off most of it."

"Yeah, I know," Craig sulks, "I'm just going to have to move out. Take this as my notice—I can send you an email if you need it in writing. I just don't know what to do. I don't have enough money to find us a new place to stay, never mind pay off the damages to the last place we had. I'm just lost here. I've hit rock bottom."

"Your brother Rab—you said he worked in oil and gas? He must have had quite a bank account before he died. You could maybe get in contact with..."

"I'm not doing that."

Craig has hung up before his landlord can utter another word. He isn't sure if it would be possible or not, but he is by no means taking advantage of his brother's death for his own gain. He still hasn't had the time to process it—Rab, taken from this world, all of a sudden with no warning. Only if someone had warned him...

Next on the phone is the council. He's got an emergency meeting in two hours with them to discuss what happened and what his options are, but he's phoning them now just to get a debrief of what said options would be and how he should prepare.

They tell him that the most likely option for him at the moment is temporary accommodation; a small, rented flat that will be his to rent for upwards of six to nine months while he searches for somewhere else or, by some miracle, works on paying off the damages to his last flat. The latter he has already given up on.

It doesn't sound great but it's better than the alternatives. As long as they have a roof above their heads, then that's all that matters for the time being. Annie's a kind, caring soul even in her young age, so Craig knows that she'll understand.

Christine would be proud of the young woman she's become.

It's a terrible thing that Annie never got to know her mother. She died during childbirth, which shook Craig to his very core. In this day and age, women shouldn't be dying from childbirth, and the possibility of it never even occurred to him. The doctors had to give her a C section as Annie didn't want to come out the other way, but upon cutting her open, something went wrong and it ended up taking her life. The doctors never fully explained exactly what happened during Annie's birth, other than it was a terrible accident.

Even now, Craig still blames the doctor that cut her open for her death. Doctors are supposed to be experts in that field—how could one possibly screw up the job and kill a woman? What a weight that must rest on his shoulders.

Some people have told him to forgive the doctor, as everyone makes mistakes, while other people have told him to go to court, to press charges, to get that doctor sent to jail and straight into hell in the afterlife, if such a thing is to exist.

But Craig couldn't. He was so depleted of all of his energy that he couldn't find the effort within him to bother doing anything about what happened. For the first two months of Annie's life, she lived in private care while Craig sorted himself out.

It seems like everyone in Craig's life seems to leave him too soon. Christine was only twenty-eight when Annie was born. Rab was only fifty-one. His parents forty-six and fifty-five. He uses every part of his being everyday to ensure that the same doesn't happen to either him or Annie. What would she do if he were to pass one of these days?

Switching his phone off for the first time in hours, Craig sighs, takes a big, appetising bite into his burger and stares off into the ball pit. Annie is having a whale of a time, but all throughout it she can't release her eyes from her father for more than a minute.

When she notices that he returns her look, she seizes the opportunity. "Come in, Dad! It's really fun. Snowy's fun to play with, but he can't move or make noises, not like on TV."

Craig smiles as she hoists her stuffed penguin into the air and catches it, throwing him into the ball pit and then searching for him again. It amazes him how kids manage to make anything fun; if he were left alone in a ball pit, he'd probably end up scrolling through social media on his phone, rueing the world and everything that happens in it.

At first he's hesitant, but then he thinks about all she's been through and of all that she will continue to go through in the next few months. He hopes it isn't longer than that.

"Alright, fine," he says, "but our hour's nearly up, remember? I'll play for a little bit."

This elates her. She gently places Snowy outside of the pit and then beckons Craig to jump in—it's a little too small for him to do that and he doesn't want to break his legs, so instead he hurls himself backwards and falls in. The balls fly into the air with his weight.

"Haha, over here!" She calls. Craig rushes forwards, hoisting Annie into the air and catching her, much to her delight. It won't be long until she's too big to do this, he thinks, and so he might as well have his fun while it lasts.

The two play for the better part of ten minutes, but to Annie it lasts a lifetime. She giggles and laughs as her usually mopey Dad crawls under the balls, hides, tries to scare her and playfully attacks her from hidden angles. They play an intense game of hide and seek, a close game of catch with the balls, and a competition to see who can juggle for the longest amount of time. Of course, Annie wins. She always does.

A worker comes up to the pit and tells them that they have two minutes left. Craig nods, and upon looking across the joint, he sees multiple sets of eyes dead set on him, some curious and joyful while others are inherently judging him. He feels a light tinge of embarrassment but then looks at Annie, who is eager to get back to it.

When their time is up, Craig remains in the ball pit for a few more moments, slowly sinking into the pit as if it's his new home. It's strangely comfortable, and if Annie were not calling out to him to get his *lazy butt* out of the pit, he may have just stayed there forever.

CHAPTER FIVE
Jess

Jess was relieved when she was released from her eight year prison sentence on parole.

It was freeing to smell air that wasn't trapped in the compounds of the prison, and it felt even better to tread on grass that wasn't in the prison courtyard. It felt liberating to know that she was back among the common folk, and that most people treated her like one of them, too. No more did she have to feel like a degenerate, or a failure.

She had assumed, of course, that her parents would take her in when she returned, and that she could begin working towards buying a house of her own. She was wrong.

Five years ago, Jess was only a young adult, two months removed from her twenty-second birthday. She had been out partying with her friends after her long-time pal Alyssa's recent engagement. It wasn't a hen party but rather the prelude to one. Regardless, she had a rowdy, debaucherous night, with hilarity and drama ensuing. At the end of the night, she wound up falling out with Alyssa over a spat about her fiancée, and so her friends got in the taxi without her—leaving her all alone miles from her parent's house.

Initially, she had driven out to the neighbouring town where the party was held herself, and was going to return the next afternoon to pick the car up. But with her friends' taxi having left without her, and her mind too distant to call one herself, she found herself back behind the wheel. Without a care in the world, no qualms, no issues.

The drive was, to her, plain sailing. But to the cars that passed her on the road, she was a massive risk, a dangerous driver. The smarter of the bunch could tell that the driver was intoxicated just from the stifled movement of the car.

Cars honked their horns. Angry voices called out to her as she flew past, hitting upwards of seventy and eighty miles an hour on a fifty mile an hour road. The road ahead of her was a fleeting rush of equidistant lines. The more focused she became, the more tired she felt, and so she deliberately took her attention off of the road to stay awake.

But when she crashed into something, she finally fell asleep.

When she woke up, she was in the back of an ambulance. Still heavily intoxicated, she had assumed that *she* was the victim, and that something terrible had happened to her. She only vaguely recalled flickering images of what had happened before she fell unconscious.

What struck her as particularly odd, in her drunken delirium, was that the response officers and doctors in the ambulance seemed scornful towards her. She thought at first that this was because she had woken them up in the middle of the night to treat her, or as if she'd phoned the ambulance for what turned out to be only a minor graze.

Jess understood a whole lot better the next morning, when news of the death came through.

Many months of legal action later, she was sentenced to eight years in prison for drunk driving and culpable homicide. When she heard the second offence said out loud, it made all of the guilt that she had suppressed rush straight into her chest, where she felt weak, frail and, most of all, guilty. And that was the verdict she got.

Throughout all of the process, from the offence to the sentencing, her parents began to distance themselves from her. They were at first shocked, and then scared for their daughter's future, but then soon became appalled and ashamed. More details came out, and that made things worse, and as time went on, Jess became more and more alone.

She hated herself more than anything, too.

What really killed her was the news that the victim, a woman of thirty-six years of age, was four months pregnant. She hadn't just drunkenly rammed into an unassuming driver and killed her, but rather destroyed all of what could've been her legacy.

Most of her friends that swore to defend her in court soon bailed, and Jess didn't blame them. She was so certain on the night of the party that they were in the wrong, false friends, and that she deserved better than them. But as court proceedings continued, she wholly understood that her friends had every right to treat her that way.

Prison was hard, but that's the point. She got out in five years instead of eight because of her good behaviour, which she had ensured to focus on.

She learned a lot in prison, too. She learned that no matter what, others in society would not forgive her for what she had done. She had also learned to accept that. She had learned to become a better person, and to treat people with respect. Even with the rowdier prisoners in her block, she would treat them with kindness, even if they relay the same kindness to her.

She improved herself in almost every manner, and yet the world truly was too unforgiving. Most prisoners that begin walking on the path to forgiveness and a more prosperous future have the support of their family behind them. But as Jess left the prison, wearing her own clothes, she realised that she had nowhere to go.

She tried phoning her parents again, in case they'd had a change of heart. They hadn't.

What really tipped her over the edge is the fact that they wouldn't even answer the door to her—she knew where they lived because it's also where *she* lived for twenty-two years. The lights would turn on, and the reflections of the TV screen flickered across the window, and yet funnily enough, whenever she'd knock or call, no one would answer.

Looking up at the remote door camera, she frowned, knowing that they'd be watching, and hoped that their minds would be changed, or perhaps convinced.

But no matter what she said or did, they wouldn't budge. This might've been her house for over two decades, but it wasn't anymore. She felt like her parents had replaced her, as if she was never truly their child, an impostor that got outed and thrown to the curb.

And so Jess became homeless. Because her parents made it clear that she was not welcome home upon her release years before it, the prison referred Jess to the council's homeless team a few months before she was granted parole. There, she received emergency housing in a local scheme estate, and a housing benefit to boot. It wasn't much to live on, but it marginally beat living in prison, so she took it.

It's a cramped, rundown little thing, her new flat. It's not hers, not really, but it is a place for her to sleep every night. It's a facade of freedom, but it's better than the streets.

It wouldn't be much of an issue if she could secure a job. But with the offence on her record, she finds that troubling, too. On some online applications, she sees the box, asking *"Have you got a criminal record?"* and debates saying no. Her time in jail wasn't for nothing, though, and so she's long past lying. She always tells the truth.

Eventually finding work in a chip shop, she makes some cash. Not a significant amount, but it's enough to help her purchase some essential items and to put towards her flat's heating, which is in dire need of a warm up. She occasionally treats herself to some fast food, which she was always told was bad for you, but she knows too well that it is better than beans on toast or the reduced steak bake's she often picks up at the supermarket.

She links up with a few of her old friends, but most of the meet ups feel awkward, as if her friends all think that she's some crazed maniac that will flip the switch at any minute. It's hard for her to enjoy herself when they're all on-edge.

It's exceedingly difficult for her to move on from the night that ruined her life and took the lives of two others. She will never be able to fully repent for her sins. The state that she finds herself in is deserved, she tells herself, but she knows, too, that she can do better.

She's got temporary accommodation, a part-time job and a few friends that might come around to understanding her again in the future.

People make mistakes. Sometimes they're minor mistakes, while other times they're dire, so bad that it feels like there's no coming back. But everyone gets a second chance at life.

Everyone *deserves* a second chance at life.

CHAPTER SIX
Craig & Annie

Craig and Annie stay at the hotel for another four nights, which virtually depletes a lot of Craig's savings over the past few months.

Five days after their house burned down, however, the two are now moving into temporary accommodation.

Craig's meeting with various members of the council went exceedingly well. It was reassuring for him to hear that there was some sort of light at the end of this terribly despair-filled tunnel; it's not a permanent home, but it's a roof over their heads. It took a few days to set up the tenancy and sign the contract, but now he's got it secured. The rent is much cheaper than his last flat, but that's because this is a single flat used for people like him—the homeless with nowhere to stay. The decrease in rent means that he can save up a little bit more to go towards moving onwards and upwards.

Their tenancy lasts for six months, and after those six months he'll have to find a place himself. It's plenty of time, and yet he feels like it won't be enough. Renting houses isn't cheap these days, and the prices seem to be ever rising. Aberdeen, all things considered, isn't that bad. He could be living in Edinburgh or Glasgow, or somewhere further down south. What if he lived in London? How utterly screwed would he be then?

Well, he figures that most people who go homeless in London leave the city and travel farther north. Searching for accommodation in London as a homeless person must be hell.

"We're nearly here," Craig assures Annie, "it's not the prettiest sight, but it's something, and we don't have to deal with those loud cars anymore."

"There's still plenty of cars here, Dad. I'm sure you'll still get annoyed."

Craig hopes she's wrong, but is also past caring. He doesn't care what the neighbourhood in Torry is like. If it's rough, then as long as he and Annie are safe, then it doesn't matter to him. Let the cars race past, let the neighbours fight and shout in the midst of night.

"Here we are," he says, "our new house is in this building."

Annie looks up at the hulking mess of brutalist architecture that stands before her. Built with grey brick, it's nothing special, but it's six storeys high. A third of the windows have been boarded up, and Annie hopes that none of those are theirs. There's a garden outside with overgrown grass and three laundry lines hanging various stranger's clothes, all still damp because of this morning's flash downpour. The smell of petrichor is oddly welcoming.

Craig removes the key given to him by the council member earlier in the morning and approaches the door. "We're on the first floor, flat 103. So unfortunately we can't go racing up the stairs like you wanted to, sweetheart."

"Aww, well I'll race you inside instead!"

"How are you gonna do that? I've got the key, not you. Not much of a race, is it?"

"I don't care. I'll get in before you do!"

The race is on, apparently, and as the two enter the landing, Annie is in such a rush to find flat 103 that she doesn't notice the thick grime forming on the handle of the stairs, or of the letterboxes that are all unlocked, half with their doors swinging open. It's still daytime, but Craig notices the flickering light and can imagine how incessant it must be at night. There's a myriad of insects fluttering about, too, and he hopes that it's just out here. If there's a whole eclipse of moths flying around the flat, he'll feel unwell.

"Over here!" Annie shouts, having found the correct door. Craig isn't sure why, but he feels a wave of fear when she shouts, as though the tenants in the building will be bothered and confront him. Scary individuals loom in his mind. It's just an ordinary council building, he knows this, but moving into a place you've never been before is always tense.

Annie presses up against the door while Craig goes to unlock it. He tells her to be careful in case she falls straight into the flat when he opens it. She says she doesn't care as long as she beats him inside. *Two can play at that game,* Craig then thinks, taking his sweet time in sliding the key into the keyhole. She might be young, sprightly and energetic, but he can win this game if he manages to bore her.

Her excitable and eager eyes squint under furrowed brows as Craig toys with her. He takes so long that once the door actually unlocks, it startles her and it takes her a moment before she pushes it open with all of her might.

"Beat you!" She says, recovering. She looks back at her Dad before even looking around at her new living space. Craig pats her on the head, smiles and looks around.

The new flat smells damp. The moment the door opened, it smelt rancid, like a room that is cleaned so thoroughly because the mess comes back the next day. The walls are stained and scratched with what looks like a brush of some sort, like someone pretended to paint it. The entire corridor is awfully small, and there are only two other rooms, those being the bathroom and the living space, which combines the living room, kitchen and bedroom all in one. Walking forward, treading on the floorboards that creak so loud that one would think that they're walking over a floor of ribbiting frogs, they enter the living space.

Like everything else in the flat, it is remarkably small in size for the two of them. The old flat wasn't massive or anything, but it was a lot larger than this. It's about fifteen square metres, but with a washing machine and makeshift bed popping out from the corners and into the middle of the room, it feels even smaller than that.

There's no room for a TV. The bed is too small for both of them to fit onto, so Craig will have to find another place to sleep. The cupboards are loose and fragile, although they don't have many possessions to store at the moment anyway. If Annie returns to school soon, he isn't sure where she would sit to do her homework. The boiler sounds like a belly rumbling.

If he could admit it to anyone, Craig would announce that he's dissatisfied. It's somewhere to stay, so he doesn't want to complain, but there's hardly enough room in here to breathe, never mind play, relax or live in.

Dropping off his single suitcase of belongings at the living space door, he walks inside, takes another look around, and then sits down on the bed. Even the slightest movement causes the bed's springs to bounce a cacophony of sound into the room. Annie sits down next to him, copying his movements. Just looking at her face, Craig can't tell how she feels.

Sitting down for the better part of two minutes, Craig begins to feel how truly cold it is in here, and feels his hand start to shake. There *is* heating in the flat, but the woman over the phone said that it doesn't work that well. Besides, even if it worked like a charm, he wouldn't turn it on as he needs to start saving money.

"So you can sleep on the bed." He says.

With no retort, Annie says *thanks.* Craig had hoped that she'd have a retort.

The first few days in the temporary flat are strange. Both Craig and Annie are unsure whether or not to feel glad that they've got somewhere to stay or to feel upset that they're now living in conditions far worse than they were before. It's bittersweet, to say the least, and so for the first days they simply take it as it is. Craig returns to work at the supermarket and works harder than he ever has before, while Annie returns to school. It's quite a bit further away from when they lived in their old flat, and so now Craig has to take her to the bus stop every morning and has to travel out to her school to pick her up. It's a little irritable, but Craig deems it better than forcing her into a new school with a new environment and new people. Trying to make new friends must not be easy, he figures.

As the days pass, however, the flat begins to take a toll on them. Craig begins working more hours at work to earn more, but it often means that he isn't home until late, and so Annie is all alone until ten, or sometimes eleven o'clock at night. She starts staying up later because Craig isn't there to tell her otherwise, and when he comes back he's too exhausted to properly enforce a bedtime upon her. He spent the first of his paychecks since the house fire to buy her an iPad to keep her entertained all throughout the night.

The problem is that, even on his days off, Craig feels totally alien in the flat. He's tried, bit by bit, to purchase items similar to those that they had in the old flat, to create the false image that they never really moved at all. Of course this is impossible to pull off, and he's left living in a small room that's pretending to be something it's not. It's a roof over his head, sure, but it's not a home, not at all.

The charade of happiness that Craig puts up for Annie is too much effort to put on after a while, and so while he joins in Annie's fun and games, he doesn't force himself to smile, or to energise himself and fully play the bit. He feels bad about it, but there's nothing he can do. He notices that Annie becomes a little more distant, less demanding of him and more independent. Independence is a good quality, but at her age too much of it is isolating.

One night, Craig decides that he will cook a proper dinner for the both of them. They've been eating ready meals ever since they moved in to save on money, but cooking up a nice meal once in a while won't do any harm. He debates upon shepherd's pie or lasagne, but after recent events he's been put off of the latter.

To raise her spirits, Craig asks Annie for her invaluable help, saying that he can't do it himself. It's more difficult than he imagined to pull her from her iPad, but after some convincing she runs over and joined him at the tiny little stove in the kitchen. After chopping up onions and carrots, he graces her with the liberty of stirring them around in the pan with a wooden spoon, but instructs her to watch out for the heat. For the first time in days, a genuine, joyful smile flashes on her face. Infectious, he smiles, too.

Cooking the dinner was fun, but eating it is still slightly awkward. The two sit on the bed with the two platefuls of shepherd's pie resting on a small stool that is acting as a table. It's difficult to bend their bodies down to eat, but Craig insists that it's better to act like they're eating properly, rather than with the plates held in their hands.

It doesn't taste the best, but that has nothing to do with the flat. Craig's never been a great cook. Rab was, though. He knew how to make almost anything — even international stuff like paella and gyros. It was always *great*. Annie knows this too. The barbecues that Rab would grill when out camping are some of her favourite ever meals.

"Dad?" She says, thinking about this.

"Yeah, what is it sweetheart?"

"Can we have a barbecue sometime soon? Like Uncle Rab used to do? If we have a barbecue we won't have to eat over the stool like this. We can eat outside!"

He isn't exactly sold on the idea, especially since he doesn't know the neighbours, but there's only one answer he can give, and so he gives it.

"Yeah, of course we can. That sounds great. Just how Uncle Rab did it."

CHAPTER SEVEN
Antoni and Zofia

Antoni and Zofia met in Katowice, Poland six years ago. They met on a *Tinder* date, and things went smooth sailing from there. Four years into their relationship, Zofia told Antoni about moving abroad, as there were more job opportunities for her there and also how it would allow her to leave Poland, which she had planned to do for years. Well and truly enamoured and in love with her, Antoni agreed, also seeing the positives in a move.

Upon entry into the country, Zofia had already been in contact with a landlord that she heard about from a friend that she met during her time studying at the University of Aberdeen. She arranged to rent this small but sweet apartment near the centre of Aberdeen and close to the nail spa that she would be working for.

At first, the move went well. Both Antoni and Zofia began working soon after they moved in and worked things out with their visas. The weather in Scotland was quite the radical departure from the weather in Poland, but Zofia much preferred the rain anyway.

Zofia knew a lot more English than Antoni did, but she soon taught him, and he enrolled in online classes, too. By the time a year had passed, he was semi-fluent. He found it a lot easier speaking and writing than actually understanding English, though, but perhaps that was just because of the thick Aberdonian dialect.

Their relationship was better than ever; both in work, earning lots of money and renovating the house that both thought could be their forever home. Their dates would get more adventurous and exciting as time passed. It started with a simple coffee date, then it was a walk up to Torry battery, and then it became full-fledged hikes in the forest. The two thought that nothing would ever go wrong in their lives—that this was *it*.

But this was not meant to be. Like most couples, there was the odd argument, but one time an argument spiraled out of control and the two fell out. Antoni flushed the wedding ring he had prepared for Zofia down the toilet. Zofia threw the ring she prepared for him into the River Don. Neither learned of the other's purchases.

For the first while, the two still remained under the same roof. But after a few more weeks of regular arguing, Zofia kicked Antoni out of the house for good.

With nothing but a suitcase in his hand and a backpack over his shoulders, Antoni suddenly became alone in the world. A hard worker at heart, he never really made any friends in Scotland apart from his work mates, but even they are closer to colleagues than anything beyond that. He managed to find temporary accommodation with the council, but that wasn't good enough. He's a middle-aged man who wants a secure life with a wife and kids and maybe a pet, too. Simply existing isn't good enough. It never should be.

A part of him knew that he could always return to live with Zofia in the future—he wagered that it was the type of argument that could go on forever, and so if he really wanted to he could live with her in debate for the rest of his life. But that's not good for either of them—he knows that—and so he swore to never return to that house.

Besides, it's her choice, not his. She was renting that flat, not him. The bills were in her name. She'd have to pay twice as much now, but Antoni knew full well that she was more than capable of doing that.

Now alone, he was faced with a great dilemma—should he stay in Scotland, remain at his job and try to find another woman? Or should he save up over the next few months, and when his temporary accommodation's contract runs out, return to Katowice?

He *could* return to Poland. At least there was security there; his family has a home that would gladly take him in. His mother and father were old and grumpy, and the idea of living with them was a bit of a nightmare, but having nowhere to stay is worse. But moving back to Poland would mean finding another job, dealing with the differences that he'd spent years getting away from, and assimilating back into Polish culture.

But if he leaves Scotland, then what was it all for? It's been two years since he moved with Zofia, and two years is a long time. One fiftieth of his entire life, and that's being generous—it'll likely be even more than that. He's built up a stable job, a stable living and a stable state of mind since coming to Scotland. He can't let Zofia evicting him tear all of that down. There's more to life than one woman. There's more houses than just one.

Antoni lingered in this middle space for months, working away and trying to figure out what his next steps would be. And no matter how hard he thought, the answer never came.

What's better? To be homeless in a country with your lifetime love just around the corner, or to have a home in a country where that love is thousands of miles away?

He couldn't stop loving Zofia—that much was true. A part of him hated her, but it was a minority of him, an insignificant amount of him. If he left Scotland, then that would mean leaving her for good, to the point of no return. And a home isn't a home without the one you love—be it your wife or your children, it doesn't matter, but living with people you don't want to doesn't make a house a home.

Zofia began to feel the same. She despised Antoni with all of her being, but a few months after he left the house, it hasn't felt the same. Half of the furniture is not in use, half of the bed is left cold at night, the bathroom feels vacant with only half of the shower products on the shelf. At times she'll switch the TV over to football, even when she has no interest in it.

She thinks about phoning him as much as he thinks about phoning her, but they're both too stubborn to do it.

The relationship is over and that's it.

Everything they've built up is done for. Those rings are never coming back.

As such, Antoni remains homeless for the entirety of his six months tenancy in his temporary accommodation. It was a dingy estate but it did what it needed to do.

In the end, he booked a plane from London to Krakow, where he'd then take the train from Krakow to Katowice. He was going home, or at least what used to be home. It isn't his home anymore—the band posters on the wall and the old race car bed are not things that belong to him but rather to the boy that he once was, before he met Zofia.

Driving to the airport, however, he drives past Zofia's house. His real home. The longer that he waits by the pavement, looking inside the windows for any sign of her, the more reluctant he feels in leaving Scotland. Before they parted ways, she was discussing renovating the roof tiles and decorating the windows, but as he sits in his car, he sees that no such renovations have ever gone underway.

It's like she left it the way it was when he left deliberately. Waiting for him to return, so that they could make it more homely together.

Convincing himself of this, he cautiously exits his car and walks up the steps to the front door. His plane leaves later in the night, and if he wastes enough time in Aberdeen, he may never reach London in time. But maybe that's what he wants?

His heart beating, Antoni knocks on the front door to his home. To Zofia's home. To their home. He isn't sure how she's going to respond to his being there, but he hopes that she welcomes in open arms, that she feels the same way that he does.

That the house will become a home again.

He knocks again and there's no response. He hears something rustling, though, and figures that it must be inside. She's thinking about it—she can probably discern his knock from any other, having heard it so many times. He knocks a third time, harder this time, to tell her that this is urgent—that she needs to answer now or he'll be gone forever. His feet become uneven, unsteady, and his stomach fills with butterflies.

It's been a minute and no one has answered. It is only then that he looks behind him, at his own car that is parked in the driveway. His car, which is parked in Zofia's parking space.

Of course. It's ten o'clock in the morning.

Zofia isn't home—she'll be at work.

If only he had left a couple of hours earlier, then maybe he could've found her again.

He walks back down the steps like a pallbearer, the weight of his life choices hanging a great weight over his shoulders. He watches his home as it fades from his rear view mirror.

CHAPTER EIGHT
Craig & Annie

Just as Craig begins to settle into his temporary accommodation, things start to go wrong.

It began with the washing machine; there must be something wrong with the pipes in the flat, as the machine would fill up with water each time it was turned on. As a result, Annie's only school uniform was soaked, and she had to go to school in her regular clothes, of which she doesn't have many as most of it burned in the house fire.

What ensued was a lengthy discussion with the head teacher of their current situation and of why Annie came dressed to school in a *Powerpuff Girls* t-shirt. Annie comes home that day all mopey, and when he asks her what was wrong she says that people made fun of her.

"There's nothing wrong with the *Powerpuff Girls*," Craig says, "most of the kids your age probably just don't know who they are. But back in my day, girls loved them."

"Yeah, and you're old." Annie retorts. It's a harmless insult but it actually hits him right in the jugular. "The girls at school think it's *cringey*."

"Yeah, well they don't know your situation, do they? They're all living at home with their happy families and a secure roof over their heads. They probably live in homes with two, maybe even three washing machines! You shouldn't care what they think."

He's trying to help, but it isn't working. If anything, it has the opposite effect. Annie sulks and throws her t-shirt to the ground, laying down on the bed top-naked. Craig sighs and collects the shirt from the ground but doesn't bother trying to get her to put it back on as he knows she's not going to. If the flat were bigger, she'd run upstairs and hide from him, but in this flat there's nowhere for her to hide. She could hide in the bathroom, but Craig just went in there and she doesn't dare go in for an hour after he's been.

Two days later, the electricity starts acting up. The fuse box downstairs must be faulty, Craig figures, as the lights would turn on and off every now and then, two or three times a day, which is relatively harmless but also infuriating. When the electric turns off, so does the internet, and whenever Annie is watching a video on her iPad, she always has the fear that it'll buffer and stop playing if the electric cuts out. Craig's fears are similar; whenever he has something cooking in the oven, he knows that there's a decent chance that it'll stop cooking if the electricity falters.

But he thinks, *at least the house won't burn down if the oven cuts out.*

Regardless, it isn't an issue that seemed to be fixable anytime soon, and after a few weeks it would switch on and off in the middle of the night, the living room light abruptly turning on even when it was switched off before the electric cut out. Many times have the pair been woken in the middle of the night, disturbed, and utterly shattered the next morning.

It was around the same time that the country reached a new low in temperature. Falling down into the minuses on a regular basis, both Craig and Annie would often fall asleep frozen, shivering sometimes and that's even with three layers and a quilt over them. Craig invested in an electric heater, but there's little room to fit it into the room and, even when it's turned on, the faulty electricity turns it off fairly often.

"I'm cold, Dad," is a phrase that Craig has begun to fear. Every night, he expects Annie to come out with it, and more often than not she does. The shiver in her voice breaks his heart every time, and he sometimes can't take it. It wears him down, and he's sure that it wears her down, too. A child shouldn't have to be subject to this.

Some nights, when Annie is resting in front of the electric heater, a thin blanket wrapped around her, he's thrown back into the night that their home burnt down. The way that she's all huddled up inside of herself, her teeth chattering and her eyes looking at nothing in particular—it's all just like that night. It's a spitting image.

The only difference is that he isn't there for her. Not all of the time, anyways, when he's working late or doing overtime. She's alone, cold, shivering and scared.

They're only a month into their temporary tenancy, and things are only getting worse and worse as time goes on. He doesn't have the money to fix these issues and even if he did there's no point in paying to fix a flat that he'll only be living in for another five months And so, begrudgingly, he accepts that he just has to suffer through it. Focus on the positives, not the negatives and try to make Annie feel the same way.

Each night after work, he begins bringing small presents for her. His boss in the supermarket understands his struggle, and allows him to take one item from the shelves each night, free of charge, and keeps it under wraps. If anyone else sees it, then his boss ensures him that he'll deal with it. He's the boss, and so his say is final.

Craig tries to mix it up each night—one night, he'll bring home a box of *Maltesers*, while another night he'll bring her a small stuffed toy from the kid's aisle. While his boss gives him free reign over the products, he does know his own limits. He can't just walk out with a new TV under his shoulders, or if he did he'd be in deep trouble.

These little gifts only have a temporary effect, though. Annie waits for her father to come home and is usually jubilant when he does, the biting cold in the room fading away for a few minutes. But the very next day, she'll wake up and feel the same as she did the day before—chilly, miserable and lacking energy. She's not the Annie that Craig raised.

The worst of all came around another week after the electricity would turn on and off during the night. One night when home alone, watching *YouTube,* avoiding her homework and waiting for Craig to come home from work, Annie heard a small crashing sound echo out from underneath one of the kitchen cupboards. Startled, she sat with her hands over her eyes and tucked herself under the bed covers.

The noise didn't go away—in fact, it got louder. Small patters of feet against the ground, a small banging sound against the cupboard walls and various small items crashing from the counter and falling onto the ground, the source of the noise seemed to be getting closer to her, and her poor little heart was beating a mile a minute.

Is it a ghost? She never really believed in ghosts, but kids at school always talk about Bloody Mary, and to tell the truth she's always been scared to try it out, so maybe she *does* believe in ghosts after all. She wants to come out from under the covers and confront whatever's making the sound, but she's too frozen to. Who knows what it could be? She could wait for Craig to get home, but she has no exact idea when that could be. It could be hours yet.

Eventually, she finds the bravery to look out. The noise comes and goes, and sometimes it sounds squeaky, like a tap that refuses to turn off. It can't be a person—she knows that—but animals freak her out as much as people do.

When she looks out, the room is pitch black. The lights have flipped off again. Her heart beats and thumps and begins to tremble. Her back crumbles her stance, and she tries with all of her might not to fall back down onto bed.

Whatever it is, it doesn't smell. All she can smell is the washing machine, which still smells like laundry detergent, and the slightly abrasive smell of mould inside the wall. She's used to both of those smells, so they don't scare her, but do ghosts even smell at all?

A shadow shutters past. She shrieks. Her eyes twitch, flicking between closing for good and staying open all night. The sleeve of one of Craig's shirts flicks upward as something speeds past it — Annie keeps her eyes locked onto this creature's position.

All of a sudden, the lights flick back on and she sees it. As she makes eye contact with it, it makes eye contact with her, and both scream and sprint to the opposite side of the room.

It's a rat!

In a way, she's relieved, but in another she's petrified. She's never seen a rat before, not in real life, anyways. Only on TV, and on TV they're always the baddies; dirty, rotten animals that need to be disposed of as soon as possible.

The two tango for quite some time, running across the ground, dodging and evading one another. Annie leaps back onto the bed while the rat slips back into the cupboard, which is where it must have come from. This fiasco continues all night, even when the rat doesn't rear its head for the better part of an hour, until Craig returns home from work.

"I'm back, sweetheart," he says, hiding something behind his back, "what are you doing up there? If you stand on the bed you might break it. Anyways, I got you this."

Craig pulls out a stuffed rat toy from behind his back. He doesn't quite understand why, but Annie screams and falls off the bed when she sees it.

"Jeez, Annie. Is it that ugly looking?"

CHAPTER NINE
Marwa

Marwa was born in Syria during a time of intense political tension. She was born into a wealthy family, and had a relatively luxurious upbringing, but the constant threat of war meant that her life was never truly secure. Money didn't provide safety.

She had just turned seventeen when the Syrian civil war officially began. Things had gone from bad to worse, and the entire country was sent into turmoil. Her family home in Aleppo was bombed, which killed her baby brother and her mother, who were both home at the time. Marwa became distraught, destroyed and defeated. Her father was in the army, and while he still lived on, she couldn't shake the feeling that he would go soon, too.

A lot of women her age began migrating to different neighbouring countries to get away from the warfare; her best friend migrated to Lebanon, while a large number of men and women that she knew who lived nearby were migrating to Turkey.

At first, she had put off migrating at all. A part of her didn't want to leave Syria, as that's all she'd known her entire life. But the damage was dire. Her home was destroyed, most of her family was killed, and there seemed to her no hope on the horizon. If she moved to another city within the country, there was always the threat of that city being bombed in the future, too. The entire country was unsafe to live in.

She mailed her father to ask for his opinion. He'd always been against the idea of migrating, even when the civil war began, and Marwa decided that his say would be final. He's the only family she had left, and so if he wanted her to go, then she would.

But Marwa never heard back from her father. He had already died in warfare when she sent that letter. She only found out four days later that he had perished.

With no one to guide her through the terrible trials of life, she decided that she would go. Her father was gone. Her mother was gone. Sticking around in Syria would not only pose a physical threat to her life, but would torment her mental state, too. And so she travelled with her neighbours to Turkey, putting the war behind her.

Six years later, a group of people living in the same complex as her began talking about travelling to the U.K. Turkey is more accommodating than Syria, but everyone always talked about the west, namely Great Britain and the United States, and of how democratic it is and of how many more opportunities there are than in Turkey.

Marwa decided that she would apply for asylum alongside her friends. In the end, it was this so-called *democracy* that enticed her, but it was mostly the idea of travelling even farther away from Syria that grabbed her. Turkey borders Syria, and so the possibility of war trailing over into Turkey was not equivalent to zero. Most people said that it would never happen, but Marwa wasn't too sure. Traumatised by what happened to her parents, perhaps, but she knew that she needed to do whatever she could to get as far away from Syria as possible.

After a lengthy process of applying for asylum and obtaining a visa, a permit to enter the country and reside there and learning of what she'll go through, she was transported, alongside dozens of others, to the U.K. Dispersed across the country, the friends that she knew well were sent to various places in England, while she was sent to Aberdeen.

She was initially relieved to find somewhere to stay in Aberdeen. It's a temporary hostel for refugees, where they stay until their asylum applications are processed, which can take from a couple of months to years. Living in the hostel with about a hundred other refugees, some from Syria, others from Afghanistan or Ukraine, she is given a weekly sum of money for her to purchase various utensils and necessities. Everyone in the hostel is supplied with three free meals per day, and while they're not the best, she isn't complaining.

It takes some time for her to assimilate into British culture; on the one hand, she experiences the weather, understands the laws and, on her walks down Aberdeen beach, begins to discover the wildlife and the different people that live in the area. But on the other hand, she's stuck in a hostel with other people in the same boat as her—it's a nice feeling in some ways, but in others it feels like she isn't *really* in Scotland, not quite yet, but rather in a liminal space between one country and the next.

She's in the waiting room. Home is a foreign concept here.

She makes a few friends in the hostel, while others she isn't too keen on. From her window, she likes looking out over Aberdeen beach, at the ferris wheel that hangs over *Codona's* fun-fair and at the kids that run towards it, dragging their mothers and father's hands along with them. She remembers what it was like to have fun with her parents.

It's not a home, but some of the people living here try to make it so. When she takes her eyes off of the ferris wheel and looks down upon the hostel's car park, she sees a group of men playing football, having moved loose bricks to make goalposts. It's a simple game, and they play it well, but Marwa always fears that the ball will hit her window and break the glass, landing straight into her room.

Like a bullet, or a bomb.

Her walks are her favourite moments in Scotland. She doesn't stray too far from the hostel as she's told not to, and so the beach and the neighbouring green spaces become her safe space, where she can walk and think without intrusion.

She's received a few nasty words from passing drunk locals, but it's like that anywhere, she hears, and it's a lot worse in other countries than in Scotland. It still pains her to see that people around her don't welcome her. Whenever she hears a sly remark or a distant insult, she feels less at home than ever before. She's a lot better off here than back in Syria, she knows, but at least back in Syria she felt like she belonged.

These things take time, an external speaker that visited the hostel said. They've just arrived here, and it's a completely different world. People take time to adjust, to adapt, and that goes for the locals that live here, too. Sometimes it takes time for people to welcome new people into their homes, but a home's a home, and a home's for everyone.

She is more than grateful for this opportunity, but her heart second guesses her mind. She feels alien, an isolated woman in a country where she doesn't fully feel like she belongs in, although she knows that such feelings are natural.

Looking at the news always scares her. It assures her that the fighting has slowed down and is now in what is called a frozen state, but she still doesn't trust it. Even if the war was to be declared over, another one very well may start again.

Months pass, and the daily routine of her life isn't much different from what it was when she first moved here. It's a little boring, and she doesn't feel like she's accomplishing much, but she knows that once her application is processed, she can apply for a job. Everyone says that it isn't easy, though, and especially for a refugee woman.

But she'll persevere. She'll have to. Scotland might not feel like her home quite yet, but simply living somewhere doesn't make it your home. Your hard work makes it your home.

The blood that you bleed, the sweat that runs down your face and the tears that are shed every once in a while—those are what make a home.

CHAPTER TEN
Craig & Annie

It turns out that it wasn't just one singular rat in the flat, but a whole mischief. Poor Annie sat in bed shaking all night, not only from the cold but from the constant threat of a rat climbing up on her and nibbling away. Craig assured her that she would be fine, but for once she doesn't trust her own father's assurances.

"Rats are scary," she says, "we never had rats at our old house."

"That's because we lived on the third floor, sweetheart. This is the ground floor, so we're much closer to the ground now. Rats usually come in through holes in the wall."

"I don't care if it makes sense!" She shrugs. "They're still scary."

It was another restless night for both of them. For the first time since moving into the temporary accommodation, Craig slept in the same bed as Annie, cradling her in his arms so as to protect her from the scary rats. It was uncomfortable for him, too, as he lay sweating all night, even in the cold. Usually he sleeps with his shirt off, but Annie insisted that he had stayed fully clothed or else she would be sick. That was a little bit demoralizing.

In his arms, she slept like a rock. It's probably the best night's sleep she's had since the house fire. The same can't be said for Craig, but this brief moment of respite allowed him to think on things, which is quite a rarity these days.

It's difficult to admit, but he has now somewhat moved on from Rab's death. He still thinks about his brother every day, kisses the portrait of him on the windowsill before he leaves for work every morning and thinks about what he would do in tough situations like this. A true heavy-hearted individual, Rab would've been able to get the two of them out of this situation if he were still alive. He would let them live in his home until things got better, or would go out of his way to lend them money and get them back on their feet and under their own roof again.

He still thinks about all of these things regularly, but the difference now is that he doesn't cry that it isn't possible. Rab died, and that's that. No amount of wishing is going to bring him back to life. He needs to take the initiative now—ensure that Annie lives a happy and secure life, just like Rab would've wanted.

With Annie fast asleep, Craig slipped out of the bed the next morning at 6AM and quietly rummaged through the cupboard that the rat came out of. Upon the realisation that there were multiple rats, not just one, he realised that he had to call someone.

By the time that Annie returned home from school that day, she came in to see the cupboard boarded up with duct tape, and several potential exits for the rats both blocked and ensnared with thick wire. When Craig returns home from work, he asks Annie what she thinks of it. His own handiwork.

"I tried calling a specialist," he says in a manner similar to a hero sharing his master plan to outwit the villain, "but the cost was too much to hire an exterminator. Plus, they'd have to go all about the building to catch and exterminate them, and I don't think it's a good idea to ruffle any feathers when we're only staying here for a while."

Annie still seems sceptical. "What did you do, then? Are the rats gone?"

"They're not gone, but I've stopped them from coming in. You won't have any unwanted guests running across the ground anymore. You might still hear them, but don't worry—I assure you that they won't be able to get inside."

"Thank you so much Dad! But how can you know for sure?"

The truth is that he doesn't know for sure. He's just living on a prayer, hoping that what he's done will be enough. But of course, he can't let her know that.

"Because Dad knows best."

That's that, then. The saga of the rats. They're still there, still lingering, smelling their food and awaiting for the opportune moment to strike. But with her Dad's say-so, Annie settles down, knowing that with him around, she's as safe as can be. She starts to see exactly how similar her Dad and Uncle Rab are. And what if the two of them were in this situation alongside him, had he not died? Well, she knows for sure that those rats wouldn't stand a chance.

But in this flat, it's one thing after another. No more than two days after sealing off the rat's possible entrance points, Annie falls ill.

It began with a fever. At school, she felt unwell, couldn't think straight and fell asleep during class. She got a stern telling off, but upon the realisation that she was unwell, her teacher forgave her, and sent her home. Luckily, Craig had a day off, and was able to collect her from the school. This was a first for him; Annie had never fallen ill, not seriously, anyways, and so he wasn't quite sure how to handle it.

It's rather difficult to heal up in the flat, too, due to the grasping cold air and the mould that lines the inside of the walls. It soon occurs to Craig that this is likely the reason that she's fallen ill in the first place—prolonged exposure to dampness and mould doesn't do the body any good, and it must be even worse for a little girl.

While he had hoped that this would merely be a short stint, that did not turn out to be the case. Over the next few weeks, Annie's illness would come and go—one night she would be bedridden, fighting back vomit, only for her to feel well the next morning. She would go to school, all would be well, and then the next morning she would be unwell again. It was a terrible game of roulette every morning, and whatever Craig bet on, the house would win.

He took her to the doctor's, but they all said what he was thinking. It's the conditions inside the house, they said. The cold. The mould. The poverty.

Apparently it's quite common amongst school children these days with the cost of living crisis, which is a fact that Craig wished he never knew. Many kids fall asleep during school, can't pay attention and see their grades decline rapidly when living situations change. All were true for Annie except for the latter part, but then a week later, after her most recent maths test, she saw her usual score of A fall down to a meagre C.

Just to test her current condition, Craig once asked her "What's seven times eight, sweetheart?"

"It's umm..." she says, contemplating, "fifty..seven? No, it's fifty-six."

Craig frowns. He wants to encourage her, but seeing your own daughter's brain decline is hard to take. She got it right in the end, but the Annie of a month ago got it much faster, and without any hesitation. It's not as serious of a matter as Rab dying, and he assures himself of this, but he still struggles not to tear up in humility.

The worst part is that Annie isn't even aware of it. Her mind's in such a declining state that her body doesn't realise that it's shutting down. She feels tired, drowsy and uninterested, but in her current state she feels as though it's always been that way.

It's like the house is sentient, and it's manipulating them, numbing them down so that it can swallow them whole, devour them, turn them into rats and wait for the next tenant.

"I advise that you either resolve the issue as soon as possible or move out of that flat entirely," one doctor advises, "her health will not get any better if things remain as they are, I'm afraid. We can prescribe you with ibuprofen, but that will only get you so far."

Craig scrunches his eyes with his fingers. "Yeah, I know. We need to move, but I just can't afford it right now. Not yet, anyways. By the time our six months are up, I should be able to rent somewhere else, but right now I just can't do it."

"I understand that it must be difficult for you, sir, but I implore you: you must take action sooner rather than later. Your daughter's health may have long-term damaging effects if she remains like this for another five months."

On his way out, Craig smashes the wall of the doctor's office with his fist in anger. He's angry at the doctor for not being able to magically cure his daughter of all the ailments that bother her. He's angry at himself for leaving the oven on that night. He's angry at the firefighters for not being there the moment the first flame erupted out of the flat. He's angry at that driver that killed Rab that night, at traffic, at cars, at all of mankind.

A kind woman walks over to him and hands him a cup of water. In the heat of the moment, he wants to grab the cup, squeeze it as hard as he can and watch as the entire corridor is splashed in the wake of his fist's might.

But he doesn't do that. Instead, he collects himself, stands upright, takes the cup of water, smiles like there's nothing wrong, and says, "Thank you so much. I needed this."

Desperate for help of any kind, Craig begins hopping around various housing agencies, relaying his story to them and inquiring into any potential opportunities that would be available to him as soon as possible. He's dressed in his best clothes, wearing his most convincing smile and veiled in the sharpest cologne in his cupboard.

Most of the firms tell him that it isn't that easy to simply procure a house to rent, and that it often takes weeks, and that there are plenty of other potential tenants that the firm may take more of a liking to. Craig finds it difficult not to lash out and cry for help. How can they turn him down or ward him off with all he's been through? It's ridiculous!

One firm tells him that they *could* get him accommodation within the week, but that he would have to sign the contract, find references *and* pay his deposit and the first month of rent within the week. It doesn't sound like it will work for him, but he feigns the fact that it could be possible, just to see how far he gets.

So the available property's monthly rent is four-hundred and sixty pounds, and the deposit is seven-hundred and fifty, which leads to a total of one thousand, two hundred pounds this week, and Craig has little under a thousand in his account. It is true that he will earn enough in his wage this week to reach the desired amount, or he could take out a loan. It won't be easy, especially since the flat is furnished, but it is technically possible.

There's a slight glimmer of hope, but upon further discussion of the references, Craig realises that it may not be possible.

"Ideally, we would need a reference from your workplace, and a reference from your current or previous landlord. In your current state, it wouldn't be the landlord of your current property as you're only a temporary tenant. It'd have to be your previous landlord—the one from the house that burnt down."

Craig's heart sinks. He knew it was too good to be true. He and his landlord didn't end on good terms, and various emails sent after their last phone call indicate that his landlord pins the full blame of the fire onto him. At what was first a civil, perhaps even cooperative relationship, has now turned into one of dismay. If his landlord had a heart, he'd give him a second chance, knowing full well that leaving the oven on to go and visit your brother in his final dying moments is hardly the worst sin that's ever been committed.

But as he leaves the meeting with the agency and calls his landlord, there's no answer—in fact, there's something even worse. The noise and indicator that the line is unreachable, that his landlord has blocked his number. If he had not been through the ringer enough already, he would smash his phone and shatter it to smithereens.

Why does the world hate him so much? It was a *mistake*. He was panicking, and not thinking straight. What right does his landlord have to *block* his number?

With that being said, Craig's not going to give up. He might not get this property, but this meeting told him that it is possible for him to obtain one. His landlord will be difficult to get to, but he believes that with time he could. And he isn't worried about his boss, as the two of them have a close relationship with one another, especially since the accident.

Later that night, during work, Craig asks his boss for five minutes of his time after his shift is over. Clearly aware of Craig's urgency, he tells him that he doesn't have to wait until the end of his shift, and can get whatever is on his chest off right now.

"So, what is it you want to talk to me about?" His boss, Marty, says, placing a steaming hot cup of coffee onto the desk. Thanking him, Craig blows on it and takes a sip.

"I've been inquiring into different possible properties, and there's one or two that look like I might be able to get. It's still up in the air, and money's still tight, so I'm not sure if I *can* go through with it right now, but I want to at least see how far I can get. You see, Annie's started to get sick because of the conditions in our flat and that's just not right, you know?"

Most bosses share the stereotype of being stern, cross and grumpy, but Marty has always had a soft spot for Craig, and it seems to have gotten even softer lately. His warm smile is not the typical boss double-crossing false sense of security. It's a real, considerate smile.

"But they say I need a reference from my boss and my previous landlord. Now I don't think my landlord's much too keen on the idea, but I was hoping you would be? I could work even more overtime if it means you are giving me a good reference."

Marty bellows and licks his sparklingly white teeth. He shakes his head in disbelief and readjusts his seating in his swirling chair before speaking.

"You don't have to work more overtime than you already do, Craig. I get that you want to make as much money as you can, but you don't want to overwork yourself. I can see that you're struggling and, I assure you from experience, that in a situation like yours, staying calm and collected is better than working yourself to the bone."

Craig stops drinking his coffee mid-sip, the cup suspended in the air. "From your experience? What do you mean?"

"I don't tell anyone this, because it sorta goes against my role as manager. You know—managers can't show any sign of weakness, no sob stories? Some firms couldn't care at all, but our almighty company wants me to put up a persona, which doesn't make much sense to me. Why wouldn't they want the PR of a manager that used to be homeless?"

Craig's mouth is wide open. He doesn't even notice it.

"Sorry, I'm rambling a bit, so I'll just get to it," Marty laughs, "It was around fifteen years ago, I think, or was it sixteen? I think it was sixteen. Anyways, I was in a similar position to you, living alone, although I didn't have a child. I still don't, funnily enough. Am I oversharing?"

"No! No, you're grand."

"OK, good. Basically, the house I lived in was built near the pier of the town I lived in, and on days with a high tide, I would always fear that water would flood my house. Sometimes it got closer, but one day the tide was higher than ever before, and a storm came from the U.S, and before I knew it I woke up and my kitchen window had broken. My floor was flooded, and the winds had breached inside and had blown all my belongings all over the place. I'll be honest, it's not nearly as bad as your situation, but I was still homeless for a few months."

"I had no idea," Craig says, "what did you do?"

"As I said, I had it a lot better than you. My mother lived only an hour away, and so I just moved in with her while they repaired my house. Since I was still working a good amount, I earned enough to pay off most of the damages myself. But do you know what helped me more than anything?"

"What?"

"I visited a support group. At first, I was distraught, and I had no idea how to go about getting my house back, or ordering for repairs or anything like that. But then I became a regular attendee at a homeless social housing support group, and we'd meet once a week, although I only went three times before my issue resolved itself. These support groups are great—I met some cracking people there, and they're all in the same boat as you, that's the magic part. They'll all give you tips, put a word in with people they know and contact local charities. The people that run these groups usually have some sort of connection to housing agencies."

"Are there any groups like that here?"

"I'm not sure, Craig, but I used to live in a much smaller town than Aberdeen, so I'm sure there will be. You don't have to listen to me, but I think it would be wise for you to attend one of those meetings before making any drastic decisions."

"Yeah, I think I will. I'll look into it when I get home. Thank you so much. But you'll still give me a reference when I eventually apply for a place, right?"

Marty rises out of his chair and yawns. "Of course I will, you idiot. You're one of my favourite employees. Now get back to work, will you?"

CHAPTER ELEVEN
Elizabeth

Elizabeth first met Gerry during their time at high school, which was many, many moons ago—back when everything was black and white. At first, during their introductory years, the two never talked much. They were both young, nervous of the other gender and of what their parents told them about love, marriage and, most intimidatingly, sex.

But they had their eyes on each other, all of that time. It started with quick, panicked glances, and then it became closer looks, lingering stares. Gerry would study harder and do all of his homework just so that he would be moved up a few seats, closer to Elizabeth.

It wasn't until their fourth year at high school that Gerry eventually found the confidence to share his feelings with her.

Of course, the two of them had spoken before, but it was never anything serious—just small talk about school, home life, sweets or something stupid and inconsequential. They always talked about their peers sexual relations with one another, as if nudging the other to repeat the same mistakes that their friends did.

And on prom night, Gerry decided that there was no point in wasting time. His friends all said the same, even to Elizabeth, which embarrassed him quite a bit but it assured him that she felt the same way, too, or at least he hoped so.

When Mr. Bates, the gym teacher, called out that the ceilidh would begin and for men and women to partner up for the first dance, Elizabeth and Gerry's gaze met for the most important time of their lives. Butterflies in her stomach, Elizabeth raced over to her childhood crush.

And from that point on, with her arms locked within his, she never left his side.

The two dropped out of high school the following year to pursue jobs in engineering and tailoring respectively, and made a good name for themselves in Aberdeen. They still lived with their parents, but with good work came good results and much needed money.

It took them less than a year to lay down the deposit for their first flat together.

When the two of them moved in, it felt like nothing in the world could stop them. They'd always have some new, exciting project on the go; be it new tiling for their kitchen or a new, sparkling car, the horizon never seemed to narrow in on them. Gerry began to get an increase in odd job requests, and Elizabeth received a pay rise for her hard work, and so both of them could never imagine rock bottom.

And they never needed to. Their house went from a council house to an outstanding achievement of infrastructure, where every architect and joiner within five miles of the house had visited and worked on at least once. Painted bright blue, it looked straight out of an American sitcom. It became a landmark site to stand in awe at for passers-by.

Amongst the cobble and granite of Aberdeen, sat a bright beacon of hope, of prosperity and of success and wealth envisioned. A lot of people didn't know who lived in the house, or what they did for a living, or if it's a couple, but they did know how successful they were.

When Elizabeth turned thirty-three, she had decided that enough was enough, and that there was no more time to be wasted.

Nine months later, the two of them married.

It really was an idyllic lifestyle, up until the end. The happy husband and wife that so many marriages predict but rarely get right. When she cooked for him on Monday, he'd cook for her on

Tuesday, and then on Sunday's they'd have a right big takeaway. Whatever he didn't eat she would, and vice versa.

They'd find a compromise on the telly, too. She would watch the nightly soap opera and, before tuning into the next one, would switch over to the second half of the football. At first he wondered why he couldn't just watch all of it, but then over time he adjusted into the routine lifestyle that they lived. Their marriage also proved that routine isn't necessarily a bad thing, either, as both of them were wholly content with their arrangements.

Of course, there were complications, as there always are. Gerry's legs started to pack in on him, and he would often have trouble walking. Elizabeth's back was killing her, and so she had to sleep at night with her nose nestled in her pillow, her back facing the ceiling. Both of them started to take daily pain killing pills, and couldn't stay up for too long.

But that's all natural with old age, and so none of it bothered them much. They complained about it, but only to make conversation. Elizabeth cared for Gerry's leg more than Gerry did and Gerry would make sure that Elizabeth's back was never strained.

We'll be together forever, Gerry once said to her, way back then.

This was only partially true. When Elizabeth woke up one morning in her bright blue house in her floral patterned quilt cover, she could feel that something was different, and yet she couldn't quite pick out what it was. She looked all over the room, but saw nothing.

She turned to wake Gerry, to ask him what it was that was wrong, but when she shook his shoulder, he was as stiff as a rock. Getting a closer look, she saw, too, just how pale his skin had gotten, and of how unsettlingly still his chest sat.

When she realised what had happened, she didn't cry. She didn't mope. She didn't even frown — not on the outside — and she didn't immediately call for help. Instead, she cradled Gerry in her arms for longer than she ever had before, knowing that it would be the last time that she could.

She was prepared for this. She knew it was coming, one day, but she was never sure which of the two of them would go first. But it was Gerry, and she was fine with that. At least he wouldn't have to see her suffer anymore — and he'd be waiting for her in heaven, too.

But it never really occurred to her just what would happen when Gerry died. She certainly didn't count on losing her house because of it, but that's what happened.

The house was in his name, not hers, and so when he passed, the house was put up for rent, the landlord searching for the next tenant. Elizabeth tried to reason with him, but the conversation only served to make things worse.

Deducting Gerry's pension and the money he'd saved, which was very little as he always made a point to *live in the moment,* would mean that Elizabeth would hardly have enough money to rent the house at all. Her pension wouldn't cover it, and nor would any of the feeble savings that she'd kept all of these years, either.

Through years of construction and decoration, it is only now that Elizabeth regrets not buying the house. It's not like they had never discussed it before, but after many years they simply decided that it wasn't necessary.

All of the tens of thousands of pounds spent on the house soon felt wasted. It would be rented out to some other, unappreciative tenant that'll dislike most of it and renovate it to look completely different anyways. In a decade or two, it might even look completely different from what it once did. If Elizabeth were to walk past it, would she even be able to recognise it? Or will it be too far gone, a long lost relic of the past that's been covered in new paint?

She never once could've imagined that losing the house would hurt her more than losing Gerry. But here she was, homeless in her eighties.

Her closest relatives lived in Australia, and while she reached out to them in hopes that they'd be able to work something out, she never heard back from them. She wasn't sure if she messed the address up or if they'd relocated elsewhere or if they simply didn't want to help her, but she was left with no choice.

As the kind young woman from the council said to her, she would be better off in a retirement home than anywhere else. The world isn't safe for a woman of her age to be wandering with nowhere to stay. Care institutions exist as a safe haven.

Elizabeth hated the idea. She couldn't think of anything worse.

And yet she had to.

The care home wasn't all bad. She received free meals, heating and television, and some of the others in the home were good fun, but she rarely focused on the positives. She took much more interest in the others, who needed help to go to the toilet, or who couldn't properly digest their dinners. She watched them and thought about how she really shouldn't be there with them, as she was still able bodied.

She got used to it, though, but she never truly found the happiness that she once had. She always thought that it was because Gerry took it with him to heaven when he passed, safe keeping it for her until she made her way back to him.

Or perhaps the house itself was their happiness—every nook and cranny of the place was littered with their history, with their words, with their presence. Spiritually, Gerry still sits in his armchair, and the kitchen table has a phantom mug of coffee sat atop it. The house was their relationship, and their relationship existed wholly within the house. The house was their one, combined and conjoined heart, beating as one.

As she's still fully in control of herself, Elizabeth is allowed out of the retirement home for lengthy periods of time, for walks or to visit some of her friends. Her own carers were at first confused as to why she was there, but when she told them, they didn't dare suggest other options, understanding that all other options have likely been exhausted.

But silently, Elizabeth isn't sitting down and taking it all in quietly. She's been asking around for opportunities to secure herself a home—she would rather die in her own company than in a home with a dozen others—and has turned up some promising prospects. She's also begun visiting a support group, which is another group with a dozen other people, although she feels much more aligned with them than those back at the care *'home'*.

CHAPTER TWELVE
Craig & Annie

As luck would have it, there *was* a homeless support group in the city and it was held once a week on Tuesdays from 7PM to 9PM. And perhaps serendipitously, the night after the talk with Marty was a Tuesday, and he had the night off.

For once it all seemed like the world was being nice to him.

Not wanting to leave her all alone in the flat if he can help it, Craig decides to take Annie along to the group meeting, too. After all, she's as homeless as he is, and perhaps rather morbidly, he knows that bringing a child with him to the group will drive more attention towards him, which will hopefully give him some spotlight to share his story.

Annie is uncertain, scared of meeting new people, even though Craig told her that they're kind people, hopefully, that will help them find a home, or at the very least assuage some of the doubts and worries that's been hovering about in their minds. He also hopes that taking her to see other people like them will raise her awareness of the situation and that she's not alone in it. Who knows? There might be another kid there that she can mingle with.

The meeting takes place in a hired office near his majesty's theatre. It must not be cheap to rent the office, even if it's only for two hours per week. This bodes well, Craig thinks, as it proves, to some extent, that whoever hosts this meeting has some degree of wealth to their name, if they're willing to pay a significant amount just to host the meets each week.

The meeting is on the second floor, which means that he has to go through reception first, and has to inform the receptionist that he's here for the *homeless* support group. It pains him a great deal as this is the first time that he's openly admitted that he's *homeless.* He's been without a home, looking for a stable roof, searching for security, but he's never once said that he was homeless. He's thought it and he's known it, but he's never said it.

The receptionist confirms that it's on the second floor. As they walk to the elevator, the receptionist flashes a sincere and perhaps pitiful smile to Annie. Craig sees it, and it makes him feel disgusted, not at the receptionist but at himself. Accident or not, he's the one that's gotten Annie into this situation. The blame falls upon him.

Entering the meeting room, Craig is one of the last there. There are about a dozen stools positioned in a circle, with ten of the twelve stools occupied. Most of the men and women waiting look in the same state that Craig is in; stable, not totally ragged, but visibly bothered, the weight of their homelessness marked in their eyes.

Before he can sit down, an older woman of about sixty approaches him. "Hi. You must be new here. I'm Dorothy, and I run this meeting. I work for a local charity, and I run this group in hopes to help aid those that struggle to find adequate social housing. I take it that you've come to the right place?"

Craig nods. "Yes, I have. It's nice to meet you, Dorothy. My name's Craig, and here's Annie. She's my daughter. She'll be six next spring."

Dorothy bends down and shakes Annie's hand. "Aww, you're a cutie, aren't you, little one? Why don't you come over here and have some shortbread? It's free!"

Annie's apprehensive, as she was told from a young age to never follow strangers, but Craig's affirming nod tells her that she should do it. Dorothy tells him to take a seat and that the meeting will be starting in five minutes. Unsure of where to sit, he decides to take the stool that's positioned next to a rough looking youngster to his left and an older, more sophisticated older woman sitting to his right. The latter turns to say hello.

"Hello there," she says, her voice as smooth as an angel's, "my name's Elizabeth. It's nice to meet you—it's always lovely to see new faces around here. Dorothy really helps you."

Craig thinks, *if she helps you so much, then how come you're still here?* But instead says, "I'm glad to hear it. It's great to meet you. My name's Craig."

A few moments later, Dorothy returns and drops Annie back off at Craig's stool. Instead of sitting on the final empty seat, she grabs onto her father's arm and stays by his side. Elizabeth turns and grins at how cute Annie is, but all her look does is make the young girl feel unsettled, out of her comfort zone and snacking on a strange sugared bread.

"OK, I think it's about time that we begin," Dorothy says, sitting down on the stool at the top of the circle so that she can get a good look at everyone, "we have three new faces tonight, so I think it'd be best if we went around the circle and introduced ourselves again, so that everyone is in the same boat. Just say your name and how you became homeless—we'll start with you this week, Elizabeth, love, and then go clockwise."

Elizabeth nods and opens the introductions. "Hello everyone. I'm Elizabeth, and I became homeless when my partner passed away. May God rest his heavenly soul."

"Hi. I'm Todd, and I'm homeless because I can barely move around my house while I'm in my wheelchair."

"Hiya, my name's Richard, and I'm homeless because I fell into a lot of debt because of…gambling and alcohol, mostly, and now I usually sleep on the streets."

"My name is Marwa. I came from Syria. I've just become…how do you say it? Free to work now that my asylum application was assessed. I'm looking for my own home now."

Dorothy forgets that she's a part of the circle too, but then quickly jolts into action. "Oh, sorry! For those of you that don't know, I'm not homeless, but I am one of the head advisors of a local charity that helps fight homelessness. I'm here to help."

"Um, what's going on…everyone? My name's Jess, and this is my first time here. I uhh, well I went to prison for culpable homicide, but now that I'm out I don't have anywhere to stay."

"I'm Cathleen. I thought my uni degree would get me a stable career, but look at me now."

"Hi guys, I'm Lynda. I'm a mother of three children, and I got laid off from my job. Long story short, I couldn't pay my bills and now I'm living with my sister."

"Zofia. I'm not actually homeless, but I feel homeless. I know you won't, but please don't laugh. My boyfriend of six years left because we had an argument, and now I'm all alone, and I am struggling to pay all of the bills alone. I'm going into debt, too."

"Alright? You all know me, haha, but for you two—Jess and," the rough looking man turns to look at Craig and Annie, "whoever you two are—people call me Lines. You can probably guess why, can't ya, haha. Well, probably no' you, wee one."

Annie hides behind her father. Lines in particular really frightens her.

Last but not least, Craig speaks up. "Hi everyone. My name's Craig and here's my daughter Annie. She's nearly six. We became homeless when our house caught on fire."

Dorothy bows her head and thanks everyone for introducing and re-introducing themselves. It never occurred to Craig just how many ways someone can become homeless—until his house fire, he had only thought of homeless people as the people you see on the streets, like Richard over there, but there's so many others out there. Craig figures that there's thousands of people in the U.K. who don't even realise that they *are* homeless.

With that, proceedings get underway. To start with, Dorothy asks the returning members to speak first, both to get the new members, Craig, Annie and Jess, comfortable with the space and to learn exactly how things work in the meeting.

Each member of the group updates the others on the progress that they've made in the past week — Todd has had no progress but apparently that's normal for him. Marwa is becoming more in line with Scottish humour and has begun engaging in meaningful conversation with a few locals. Zofia has sold some of her antique household ornaments to make some money and has cut down her broadband deal to spend less. Lines is now three weeks sober (although Dorothy seemed doubtful) and Elizabeth is still overcoming her husband's death.

Of all members, however, Lynda has the biggest announcement of all. Due to her savings over the past few months, she's been able to locate and get into contact with a housing agency, recommended to her by Dorothy, and is aiming to move in at the end of the month. She's also picked up some part-time work in a café. The room is full of applause.

Craig isn't sure whether or not to feel glad for the woman or to envy her. Her situation is perhaps the most similar to his, and he's also looking into accommodation. But unlike him, she's seemingly successful, and is on the path upward. Then again, who knows how long she's been homeless for, while Craig's only been without a home for a month.

Up next, Dorothy beckons both of the newcomers to share their stories. Jess goes first, relaying her story of how she went to prison and of how she has redeemed herself—she really wants to make this clear, which makes sense to Craig—and of her current situation. It's a sad story, but everyone here has a sad story, and Craig's no different. He finds it difficult to listen and engage with Jess's story because he's so pressed about his own, about what he will and won't tell the others. Should he mention the oven? What about Rab?

The two dozen pressing and prying eyes convince him to do so. To tell everything. After all, if he doesn't tell them everything, then he might not gain their full trust, and without their trust, then what is he here for? He's here to connect, to learn. Not to lie.

When he's done telling his story, everyone makes their condolences known. Elizabeth even starts to cry, which Craig initially thinks is a bit over dramatic, but then thinks about how she's crying over *him* (or Annie, more than likely), and of the image that paints of him. He's sure that Elizabeth cries over everyone's story, but at this moment he feels special.

"OK, that's your account of the story, Craig," Dorothy says, "Now what would you say, Annie? Don't feel pressured to talk if you don't want to, but could you tell us how you've felt ever since your house burned down? You can be honest with us."

Craig expects Annie to be timid, but for once he's wrong. Perhaps it's because of the open nature of the meeting, but Annie wastes no time in speaking her mind.

"I don't like it, but I know that it's not Dad's fault," she says, looking at Craig, "and I know that things are going to get better. I don't like eating on a stool, and I don't like being all cold when I sleep, but Dad's been working his butt off to get us a house. The rats in the house really scare me, but Dad kept them out, and now I don't have to worry about them, and…and…" her thoughts seem endless, running like a well-filtered stream, but come in such thick waves that her mind stops temporarily. Eventually, she blurts out, "Can you please help us find a home? That's why everyone is here aren't they?"

There's silence but it isn't awkward. Everyone looks at Annie as if she's some sort of divine messenger sent from the heavens. Craig's a little embarrassed, flushed, but sees the smiles on everyone's faces and thinks against scolding her. After all, she was just speaking her mind, and it's nice to see her do that nowadays, instead of becoming a recluse.

"You're so well spoken, Annie, dear," Dorothy says, "are you sure you're six?"

"I'm not six, I'm five! I turn six in April."

"Ah, yes, that's right. My apologies."

The depressive atmosphere that filled the room has now all but completely vanished, gone with the wind as Annie's bright personality and Lynda's amazing news has brought everyone to higher spirits. In only an hour, Craig understands why Marty was helped so much by a group like this — on a spiritual level, you feel at ease here.

For the final fifteen minutes of the meeting before adjourning for the week, Dorothy gives some tips to certain people, and diverts her attention to Craig at the very end. She gives him nothing definitive, but very many sources of reliable information and important phone numbers and emails to keep in close contact with, mainly charities that help fight against homelessness and various helplines and leasing agencies. He recognises most of them as the agencies that he inquired about earlier yesterday, but there are some new ones in there, too.

It's nothing that's going to immediately change things, but it sure is a lot of help. He thanks Dorothy and assures her that he'll be back next week. Dorothy returns the gesture.

On his way to the exit door, he's stopped by Lines, who still unsettles Annie. All of the people at the meeting presented themselves relatively well despite their situations, but Lines is quite different. He's a former drug user that still looks and acts like he takes drugs daily, which is quite harsh but it's true. His eyes are all over the place and his jaw is loose, his flat black cap hiding a messy shrub of greasy hair. He seems nice enough, but his exterior demeanour is the type that people like Craig tend to avoid.

"You mind if I walk with you, mate? I only live doon the road."

Craig is at first unsure. He's dodgy-looking, but surely he wouldn't try anything immediately after a meeting to help homeless people? Surely no one would stoop that low, to pick on those who're already at rock bottom?

Craig has a little bit of hope left in humanity, and so he accepts his offer, walking down the street with him, en route to his car. Lines seems far more interested in him than he is Annie, which is a reassuringly welcome sight.

"You know, it's a shame us homeless folk have such a bad reputation. Or some of us do, at least, but probably not you, mate. You're still new to this stuff."

Craig sighs. "Yeah, I suppose. But I hope I'm not homeless for long."

"Ach, none of us do, mate. But sometimes we are. That's the thing—the longer you're homeless, the more people look down on ye, you know what I mean? You sleep on the streets, you're no better than scum. You stay with your relatives for too long? You're becoming a burden. You live in one of those temporary places like you are? Then you're surviving off of benefits and the council. We're all in deep shite, mate, but people that haven't been through what we've been through just dinna get it."

In all truthfulness, Lines is talking a lot more sense than Craig had imagined. Perhaps looks really do deceive. As the pair reach his car, an idea crosses his mind, and he isn't sure if it's a great idea or a terrible one, but he follows his gut.

"You might be right about that one. Here, why don't you come over to mine for a little bit? I want to hear your full story. I've got some beers in the fridge."

"I'll take ye up on that, mate, if it's no bother. But I'll have to say no to the booze—I'm three weeks sober, remember? No booze, no eccies."

Craig smiles and unlocks the car. "That's what I like to hear."

CHAPTER THIRTEEN
"Lines", or Zachary.

Before he became addicted to drugs, Zachary was a high-stakes gambler, and quite the character in his local area. Leaving high school without a stable job, he started using his football expertise on his eighteenth birthday to win himself a boatload of cash on multiple betting sites, mostly focusing on football accumulators that would earn him hundreds of pounds at a time. His parents at first frowned upon this lifestyle of his, but once he began winning consistently and raking in thousands of pounds, their tone soon changed.

It is needless to say that he became a local legend. If you visit any casino in Aberdeen and ask about a man named Zachary, or mostly known as *Lines*, then you'd be hard pressed not to find someone that either knows or knows of him.

He'd always had an addictive personality — it was a trait known to his family from a young age, where he'd crave the same foods, play the same games over and over and stress over the same equation in school over and over again, hours after he'd arrived at an answer.

He rode on his high horse for around three years, until his twenty-first birthday, where a few of his accumulator lines failed to come in in a row. Of course, as a gambler it is natural that not every bet wins, but for six bets in a row to lose, Zachary had never felt such repeated defeat before. He felt humiliated, and after every loss, he'd convince himself that it was a fluke and that he'd win the next one, but to no avail. Loss after loss after loss.

This really got to him, and so he hit up his friend and entered the drug dealing business as an escape from gambling. He'd taken his fair share of class A drugs over the past few years, and so he believed that he would be well trained to sell the stuff—it's a much more reliable source of income than gambling, he soon thought.

At first it went well, and for the first six months he netted more cash than he ever made gambling—soon, his nickname *Lines* took on a whole new meaning.

He became well known in an entirely different circle of people. From avid gamblers to the drug dealers and the drug consumers of Aberdeen. Admittedly, he felt a little sleazier dealing drugs because of the fact that it's illegal, but the money spoke for itself.

Everything was plain sailing until both of his parents died. Often, that seems to be the downward spiral for lots of people out there. His mother had died of a heart attack at work one day, and his father passed away in his sleep just over a week later. It's funny how couples die close to one another like that sometimes, except Lines wasn't laughing.

Utterly devastated and thrown into great despair, he began indulging in the drugs that he sold, and so he would not only lose out on profits, but his suppliers began to distrust him, too, and so the entire operation began to crumble.

Six months later, he no longer dealt drugs, but just consumed them. He wasn't sure what was worse, him then or him now, but when he was on a high, he didn't care.

It wasn't long until he sold his house. He bought the house himself with his own gambling winnings—his mother and father were so proud of him. But then he went and threw it all away, and no more than two years after selling the house, he spent two-thirds of the cash he received for it on drugs. A kind, sharing man, he would make a habit of buying some for his mates, too, and they quickly became reliant upon him.

But with no source of income, he eventually ran out of money and ran out of drugs. With no place to stay and no living family that would willingly take in such a severe drug addict, he hopped around from his friend's flats, only staying until they'd had enough of him and kicked him out. It's OK, though, as he knew deep down that they'd always welcome him back if he brought some goods with him.

He lived this lifestyle for another three years. His physical and mental health deteriorated greatly, and he soon became indistinguishable from the man that he once was. He always mingled in illegal activities and lived in the nightlife of Scotland, but that's all he became—the alcohol in his stomach, the needle piercing his veins.

Whenever he entered a casino, no one would recognise him anymore. His face had aged twenty years in the past five, and his pale skin blemished more blue than cream. If someone did recognise him, they'd shake their heads and mope.

What've you done to yourself, Lines, they'd usually say.

His life became a true and utter mess. His friends, fully aware of his routine, would begin to kick him out of the house the same night that he visited; very rarely was he permitted to sleep over and stay a night or two. Things would often get violent, and most of the time it would be he who ended up in hospital, not them. His body strength was next to nothing, fully falling in line with the allure and spell of the drugs that controlled him.

Soon enough, all of the police working in Aberdeen knew of him and of his backstory as a casino God and of a drug dealing Judas. But when they're called to arrest him, it often has nothing to do with drugs, or nothing to do with gambling.

The last time that he was arrested, he was caught stealing a beef steak from *ASDA*. He thought he was clever, ripping the QR code off of the packet and sprinting out of the front door with it, avoiding the alarm of the item scanner.

Maybe if he was more subtle about it, then he might've gotten away with it.

It was only after his fifth arrest that the police began to give him some guidance to get his life back on track. Having suffered many fines for his offences, he couldn't afford to rent any flats, nor did he meet the requirements to apply for benefits, either. And so, while continuing to hop around various houses, the police gave him various meetings and groups that he could join for rehabilitation. Forced to go to all of them at least once, he at first despised it, the comedown of life, and wanted nothing more than to take another hit.

But after a while, he started to get it. Instead of drugs, or alcohol, or gambling, he became addicted to getting himself back on track. Listening to all of the sob stories at the homeless group and at alcoholics and drug anonymous, he began to realise that perhaps living life on a constant high is, in reality, the lowest of the low.

The longer that he went without taking any drugs, the more he truly felt how alone and unhappy he was in life. He no longer yearned for a hit, but for a warm, cosy bed, and a home that he could call his own. It was challenging for him to accept just exactly how much he had thrown away in the pursuit of drugs; first his home, and then all of his money, and finally all of his friends, and his dignity, too. He had it all, but now he has nothing.

He's done with the accumulator lines.

He's done with lines of cocaine.

Now the only line that he follows is the straight line of sobriety.

It's not going to be easy; he spent the past five years tearing everything down, and he wagers that it'll take a lot longer than that to get it all back. But in essence, he's still in his twenties, and his entire life is ahead of him—he may not have been able to say the same if he had kept abusing drugs for momentary, flickering surges of joy and ecstasy.

True ecstasy is found in the home; in the warmth of a loved one's arms, or in the simple moments in life. Lunch with your friends. Your new clean clothes. Your warm bed.

CHAPTER FOURTEEN
Craig & Annie

After tucking Annie into bed for the night, Craig and Lines spent the better part of three hours talking and drinking in Craig's parked car outside. The flat is far too small for the two of them to talk without waking Annie up, and so the car had to suffice. Craig still wasn't entirely sure of Lines at first, but by the time he left, he recognised him as a formidable man that managed to turn his life around against impossible odds.

"You've got this, mate," a sober Lines says to a tipsy Craig, "not to say *woe is me* and all that, but I had it quite a bit worse than ye did, mate, and even I'm on the mend. If you keep that head of yours on tight and keep asking around for flats, you'll be golden. But it's not nice seeing that girl of yours be affected by all of this."

"You're telling me," Craig laughs without smiling, "I feel an ounce of guilt every time I look at her. She's a strong girl—stronger than me, sometimes—and she'll push through it, but her health isn't getting any better. She was up and at em' tonight, but tomorrow? Who knows. It worries me every single night."

"Hey buddy, if I had to bet on it, I'd say that you're worrying too much. Sure, her health's taken a dark turn, but it's nothing fatal, is it? In the end, she'll get better."

Craig chugs the rest of his bottled beer and seals his lips shut so that it doesn't all come crashing out with his joke. "I don't think *you* should be betting on anything!"

"Good one, mate—I've never heard that one before."

Many chortles and guffaws later, Lines departs and heads home. Craig offers to drive him but then remembers that he'd been drinking. It's just a small thing, and he never would have driven him under the influence anyways, but the fact that he considered it for even a split second truly pains him. Has he learned nothing from Rab's death?

Lines says his goodbyes and says that he'll see Craig at next week's meeting. Craig welcomes the idea and, once Lines is well out of view, he falls back in his seat and relaxes. He's not drunk alcohol in a while, and if it was not irresponsible to leave Annie all alone in the flat, he might have even fallen asleep here. It's warmer, at least, but a little bit more packed.

The next morning, he feels a little hungover, which makes him feel a little shameful. Back in his glory days, even a dozen pints would fail to make him hungover, but now all it takes is two, it seems. *Getting old's scary*, he thinks.

Maybe Annie's right—he *is*, actually, old.

That morning is eerily quiet, but Craig assumes it to be a result of his hangover, as it's been so long that he thinks that he's forgotten how it felt. His sickness isn't helped by the shower hose breaking in two, spraying two separate streams of water, one left and one right. He groans, and as he tries to pick it up, it sprays all over the wall and onto the sink.

His towel already soaked from the splashing, he switches the hose and thrusts it down into the tub. That's another thing that needs fixing now.

He dries off and gets dressed, but as he bends down to grab his socks resting on the bottom of the bathroom shelf, he notices strange markings on the inner basin of the toilet seat. At first he thinks that it's grime, but upon closer inspection he sees small undigested lumps of food and trails of a pale yellow liquid. Now that he sees it for what it is, he smells it, too.

Rushing to get dressed, he almost falls over and smacks his head against the toilet seat, but manages to keep himself standing upright. The bathroom is so small that he all of a sudden feels trapped, as though the room is closing in on him. As he slides his boxer shorts onto his damp groin, he deems himself dressed enough to leave the bathroom.

Frantically, he sprints into the living space, shouting "Annie! Annie! Are you OK?"

Annie is laid out on the bed with her limp arms covering her face. When he first woke up, he assumed that she had been sleeping, but now he sees it for what's really happened.

She's passed out! Oh no. Oh no, oh no!

Craig isn't sure what the proper procedure is but at this moment he couldn't care less; he grabs his daughter by the shoulder and shakes, calling her name over and over. When she doesn't budge, he moves her arm from her face and picks her up, bobbing her up and down like he did when she was a baby, as if that will bump her back into consciousness. When it doesn't, he rushes over to the sink and flicks water onto her face. No luck.

What could have possibly happened? She's still breathing—thank God for that—but she's still unresponsive, and nothing seems to wake her. Is her illness worsening?

For the first time since Rab's death, Craig rushes straight into A&E, his five year old daughter cradled in his arms and an endless array of calls for help streaming out of his mouth, spraying out in every direction, a broken shower hose. Nurses and attendees rush towards him, skipping past a few unfortunate souls that have been waiting, and take Annie from his grasp. A nurse asks him what happened while speed walking to the treatment room. Struggling to think and failing to find the right words, he just says it as it is.

"The house did this," he says, "our dingy flat that we've been living in for the past month, ever since our house burned down. I think it's mould, or something."

"OK," the nurse says, "we'll take it from here."

The forty-five minutes that Craig waits are perhaps the most excruciating moments of his life. It's a terrible thought, but at least with Rab's death, it was plainly obvious upon the first glance of his half-torn, ripped apart body that he was going to pass. But this has so many layers of uncertainty to it—for one, he isn't sure whether or not the mould actually caused it or not, or if she's actually in fatal danger or not.

He knows that it's unrealistic and unlikely to boot, but if he were to lose her, then that'd be it for him. All the progress they've made would go down the drain. No house will become his home if Annie isn't there with him. It'll be empty without her.

His heart will empty without her locked tight inside.

When the nurse returns to debrief him, it's bittersweet news.

Here's the good part: Annie's alive and well, and she's not going to die anytime soon. The negative part, though, is that it *was* the mould that did that to her. It might have started with a fever, but the doctor tells him that she's begun experiencing respiratory issues due to the mould in the flat, which has been causing her to suffer through shortness of breath. The doctor insists that she remains in hospital overnight and that Craig either goes home and sorts the issue out or moves out entirely. Essentially, he's parroting what the previous doctor said before, back when it was only a fever.

But this time it's urgent—it's a call to action, a warning that living in the flat for much longer *can* lead to her death, as horrifying as that fact may be.

He agrees with the doctor's offer to keep Annie hospitalised overnight, as there isn't any alternative that won't severely make her condition worse. At least here she can heal and lay down in warmth for the night.

Craig doesn't have the time to sit around leisurely, waiting for her to come back out—he needs to do what the doctor says and *act*.

The first thing that springs to mind is posting on social media. Usually, Craig rues this kind of thing, as he thinks that no one really needs to know anything, and the people that want everyone to know everything are usually just attention seekers. But under these circumstances, he knows that it would be a worthwhile endeavour to update his status.

Had a shock this morning. Annie's in hospital due to repository issues because of the mould in our flat. Does anyone know of anywhere we can stay for a little while? The longer the better. Thanks.

It makes him cringe while he types it out, but sometimes you just have to bite the bullet and move on. There might be someone out there, between his three-hundred friends or false friends on *Facebook* that may be able to help them out. Who, he has no idea, but there must be.

He also slides Dorothy from the meeting a quick message, filling her in on everything that has happened this morning, and of what he's planning to do. She replies almost in an instant, wishing Annie well and asking him to keep her in the loop—if he needs anyone to look after Annie in hospital for a while, she can lend her time.

Next, Craig drives to the supermarket where he works, not to get a shift in but to purchase various cleaning supplies for a deep clean. He purchases all sorts of tools, from metal scrubbers to spray bleach to elbow grease to a twenty-pack of sponges, to deodorisers to magic spray cans that supposedly eliminate mould. When he leaves the supermarket, he's carrying with him a basket of over twenty items, all adding up to the better part of sixty pounds.

Between one in the afternoon and eight o'clock at night, Craig gets to work on the flat that isn't really his. He gets every single corner of the flat, pushing cupboards and moving the counter out from the wall. Unfortunately this comes with the risk of unleashing the rats into the room, but if that happens, he'll deal with it when it comes to it.

He sprays all of the kitchen tiles. He hoovers the room not once but thrice, even though he knows that there shouldn't be any mould in the carpet, he thinks, and then hopes.

He makes sure to scrub the windowsill over and over again, and to line the walls with the same treatment—mould often grows from inside the wall, and so he tries with all of his might to scrub it clean, to eliminate any source of anything relatively fungi related from creeping back into the room. It might be a feeble attempt, but he gives it all he's got.

By eight, he's famished, drenched in sweat and worked harder than he's ever worked before. The flat is now sparklingly clean, and yet there's something about it that still looks dirty. He's not satisfied with it, but he knows that that's no fault of his own. No matter how clean the flat may be, it's not his own, not his home, and so it'll never truly look right.

Will this be enough to lessen the influence of her symptoms? To tell the truth, Craig doesn't think so, but he's given it all he's got.

After showering, he opens his mobile for the first time since three o'clock. His *Facebook* messenger inbox has five messages, mostly from distant relatives or from colleagues sending their regards for what happened and wishing Annie a speedy recovery. But one message stands out above all the rest—it's from his old friend from high school, Dean.

Hi Craig, long time no see.
I saw your Facebook post, and I'd be willing to let you and Annie stay at a private complex of mine for a while. We can meet up tomorrow and talk about it if you'd like?

CHAPTER FIFTEEN
Cathleen

Growing up, Cathleen was a prodigy child. She was the dux pupil, the child of the future.

She was the next big thing.

She got five A's at higher level in high school, three A's and a B at advanced higher level, said the B was because she fell ill before the exam, which was partially true. She travelled down the country, from the Orkney Islands to the University of Aberdeen, where she studied philosophy as an undergraduate student. At first, she found it ropey, out of her comfort zone. Her excellence would sometimes falter, and she'd be graded at B or C level regularly.

But she found her groove—she always did. By the third year of her study, she once again became the salt of the Earth. Always the highest in her course. By the time that she graduated, she had earned a first class honours degree only because there was nothing else better than that. If there was an award for ultimate excellence, she would've won it.

The whole world was ahead of her. She could go anywhere, meet anyone, and become anything that she wanted to be, even outside of the realms of philosophy. Some of her friends envied her, while the more self-centered pitied her. Neither ever bothered her because what was she to be bothered about? How truly, utterly brilliant she was at everything?

Her prospects after graduating were through the roof. Unfortunately, so were travel prices, accommodation, postgraduate education, and, above all else, the cost of living.

She could go anywhere in the whole wide world, and yet she ended up back at her parents house. Back to where it all began—back to square one.

At first, it didn't bother her. She was just popping back home to visit her parents. They raised her, and so she owed it to them to spend some time with them. Mingling with her old friends from high school and returning from the big city, she felt like a famed celebrity.

She would drink her lungs to their fullest capacity as a celebration, uncaring for the consequences because she was always going to reach the moon. She got back into her previous relationship with her boyfriend, who she broke up over due to the long distance nature of their relationship prior. She began to wear her old clothes that had collected dust, to eat off of old plates and to reread books that she hadn't read in years.

She got herself a job—only for a little while, she said—and worked her butt off for money, to which she would save and save until she could finally soar into the skies.

Of course, the weekend would come around, and she'd spend a little, here and there, but she still had more in her bank account than she did at uni, so what harm is there in that?

Her friends would call her *Aristotle*. Her parents would joke at the dinner table, praying before they eat but instead of a prayer they would recite a quote from *Plato* that they found online, although they clearly didn't understand what it meant. Her boss would ask her *what's the point in studying philosophy? We're a Chinese takeaway*. And, most importantly, she would ask herself, *what am I doing with my life? What was it all for?*

She never found the answer, and still hasn't. But she isn't much looking for it anymore, and she doesn't much care to find out, either. She once had an interest in enquiring about Oxford University, but now the idea of it makes her laugh. While she had originally planned a mega list of over two-hundred philosophical books, papers and manifestos to read, she now finds much more comfort with her nose between a gossip magazine.

It's the same, really. Philosophy and gossip, morals and ideologies and scoops and scandals, all of it's about the human condition.

There's no difference. Not at all.

After six months, her parents started to berate her about it. On one hand, they're proud of her, of what she's accomplished and of how she's secured a stable job that pays decently well and provides for the community—everyone loves a drunken Chinese, after all. But on the other hand, it loomed in their minds that her degree seemed to amount to nothing—her father had doubts when she first travelled to Aberdeen, and now they seem to have been proven right. If the Cathleen of four years ago would've known that, then perhaps she would've given up, or pushed even harder, or have taken a different route.

In the end, though, none of that would've mattered. If you have no money in life, then you're pretty much screwed. As each day passes and her monotonous, routine life drones on and on and begins to irritate her, she starts to believe that.

Not long after, her boyfriend breaks up with her because she's *too boring,* which she thought was ridiculous, and her parents thought was ridiculous, and her friends thought was ridiculous, and it *is* ridiculous, but it happened, and that's what he thought, and it nearly sent her over the edge.

They had plans to move into a new house together. They'd put both of their savings towards it—most of it was his. It was only a small prospect. Something to get excited about, to work towards. But now that's all down the drain. She's at a deficit, and her parents are unwilling to lend her money because they've lent her plenty already.

She has the security of her hometown, the security of her parents, of her friends and family, and yet she feels insecure and out of place. She doesn't belong here—she's known this since she was a child, when everyone told her that she'd be the next Einstein, a future millionaire, or a future politician. She's never belonged here because everyone always talked about her as though she belonged on another planet.

She was naive to think that this was all true. She never could've gone to Cambridge or Oxford or Harvard. She was never going to win the Nobel Peace Prize.

About two years in what she could only describe as purgatory, she finally saved up enough money to move out of Orkney. She wasn't going to the moon, or to New York, but to Aberdeen, and that was good enough.

Even house prices are rising exponentially, and so she isn't even renting a flat on her own—that would cost too much, and with no one she knew at university still residing in Aberdeen, she had no one to contact for help. In the end, she moves into a temporary flat for twelve months, while she works at her new job and saves up to find a new place.

Ever since leaving university, Cathleen has never known a life without homelessness. People always called Orkney *home*, and she did, too. But after living in Aberdeen for four years, studying and living by her own accord, Orkney isn't her home anymore. Nowhere is—her home lies at the end of her knowledge, wherever it takes her.

But it has crash landed, now, and she's lost. Living with her parents provides security, but it's all a facade—she's still homeless, even if she lives with them, leeches off of them.

This temporary flat depresses her. It's old, the floorboards creak and it stinks of something foul. She's never lived in conditions like these, and it revolts her, not only due to the physical space in which she inhabits, but because of what she's become.

She went for the moon and ended up floating, stranded in space. Looking for a home that could very well be light years away, in another impenetrable galaxy.

CHAPTER SIXTEEN
Craig & Annie

The day after Annie is discharged from her hospital bed, Craig tells her that he has a big surprise in store for her—and this time, it's not a stuffed rat, or a chocolate bar. Still feeling a little unwell, she's welcome to the idea of a gift but can't find the mental strength to figure out what it could possibly be. A friend for Snowy, maybe? Or a new bow for her hair?

She can't really think, but for once Craig's grateful for that. It'll make the shock on her face even bigger when she sees it. Even *he* is a tad excited to see it with his own eyes.

It seems odd to her that this gift, whatever it is, is so far away from the flat. Craig's been driving for about an hour, and shows no signs of stopping. Is he taking her to a resort that she's never heard of before? Are they going camping, like she and uncle Rab used to? The latter would usually sound fun, but she isn't much in the mood for building a fire.

"Here we are, sweetheart," Craig says, his excessive jubilation marked on his face, "welcome to your new home…for the time being."

Upon the mention of the word *home*, she jolts up in her seat and stares out of the window.

The car pulls into the driveway of a staggeringly tall, four-story mansion in the middle of nowhere. Its makeup is something straight out of the Victorian era.

"Woah!" Annie says, exasperated. "We're staying here?"

"Just for a little while, but yeah, we are, sweetheart." He parks the car right next to another much fancier looking car, long, thin and pitch black — the sporty type. "I'm not sure for how long, but hopefully it'll be until we can get a place of our own."

Annie is out of the car before Craig is. She looks all around in wonder, at the graciously expanding green garden to the perfectly trimmed shrubbery to the tall, authoritative gates with spikes at the top and, of course, at the mansion itself. Her eyes glisten as if she's seen a shooting star. She looks to her Dad in disbelief.

"This is ours?"

Craig is awestruck too, but he tries to act cool in front of his daughter. Walking on the dirt path, he kicks dust into the air, his hand buried in his pockets and making sure to to only glance up at the building every now and then, as if it only mildly interests him.

"Your Dad knew this guy called Dean in high school—around fifteen years ago—and I hadn't heard from him in years. Maybe seven, eight years? A long time ago. When you were ill in hospital, getting treated by all of those kind nurses, he messaged me for the first time in ages—I was shocked, really, but it felt good to hear from him again."

"What? And he just gave you a mansion?"

Craig chuckles. "No, obviously not, you silly billy. We met up yesterday morning, just before I picked you up, and we had coffee together. I told him all about our flat and the mould and what it was doing to you, and so he offered us the chance to stay in his mansion while I work on getting things better for us."

"He sounds really nice."

Craig nods his head and stares at the ground. There's a little bit of tension here, and Annie doesn't really understand why, but she doesn't care much either, what with the mansion in front of her, which is about to be her own. She starts forward and sprints to the entrance door, calling for her Dad to follow. Stumbling over himself, he ensues chase.

Even the door to the mansion is inherently fancy. Embroidered with emblems of lions and dragons, Craig isn't sure what it means, but it sure looks prestigious. Annie thinks it's cool, and proclaims to her Dad how it feels like they're entering a magical fantasy castle. Before she knocks, Craig pushes gently ahead of her and knocks instead.

"You're right to be happy, sweetheart, but know that you have to be on your best behaviour if you want to stay here, now. You wouldn't want to upset Dean, would you? If you upset him, then he might not let us stay here for much longer."

Annie nods and furrows her brow, determined to defend her position as heir to the castle, or whatever story she's made up in her head. Craig's look is a curious one.

Pulled by a lever inside, the two gigantic sliding doors creak open, and a cloud of dust emits from the weight of their movement. Annie thinks it's the best thing that she's ever seen with her own two eyes. Craig thinks it's all a bit extra.

"Welcome, welcome!" Dean calls, walking towards the pair of them. "I hope that your travel here went without issue. You're a little later than I imagined…?"

"Sorry, we got lost." Craig says. "It isn't exactly easy to get here, is it?"

Dean, a tall and slender man with circle rimmed glasses, the type that John Lennon often wore, is as handsome as he is cheesy. Shrugging off that the pair got lost with an over enthusiastic *sorry about that* shrug, he diverts his big, overzealous smile to Annie, who for the first time in over a month feels totally safe in the vicinity of a stranger.

"You must be Annie. Craig here's told me a lot about you," he looks back and forth between the two, "my, you both look awful alike. Are you two related?"

"He's my Dad, dummy!"

There's laughter all around. Giddy laughter under a set of growing teeth. Polite laughter under fat, moisturised lips. Muted laughter under a thin, disingenuous smile.

Without much stalling, Dean beckons the two of them to follow him as he gives them a short but in-depth tour of the premises. First off, there's the courtyard, which is larger than two football fields and is complimented by a stone water fountain in the middle. Then, heading inside, there's the entranceway, with enough coat hangers to fit an entire army battalion. Heading inward, Dean showcases the lounge and the living room, which are two separate things, the kitchen, the dining room, the pantry, the laundry room, the games room, the first, second and third toilet, the four bedrooms, all out of use, and the back garden, fitted with an outside spa and sauna. It's all really impressive, and Annie prances around like she's at Disneyland, Dean the stand-in for Mickey Mouse.

While he's trying not to show it, Craig is amazed as much as Annie—perhaps even more so, given his past connection with Dean. This is the type of home that Craig always dreamt of when talking about the future with Christine, before she passed. A fairytale mansion out in the middle of nowhere, away from the fumes emitted from cars and in urban decay.

Dropping Annie off at the games room to play for a while, Dean sits Craig down at the dining room table, sitting opposite one another. Dean offers Craig a glass of wine, but he refuses and asks if he has any beer instead. It shouldn't have surprised him when Dean came out with a whole plethora, asking, *which one would you like?*

"Who would've thought that this would be happening all of those years ago, eh? You, living it up in a mansion, and this isn't even your main home. Meanwhile, I'm homeless, drifting from one place to the next because I let lasagne burn my house down. If you told me this would be happening back in high school, I'd laugh in your face." Unsure of how Dean will take that, he adds, "No offence, of course. I'm really happy for you."

"Yeah, you're right. Who would've thought? I know I wouldn't have. I'm not sure if I even truly believe it now, after owning this estate for five years."

Craig's eyes are torn between two worlds; the past and the present, intersecting one another, existing not separately but both at once. He sees the current Dean, and all of his luxuries, but he also sees young Dean, who sat next to him in History class.

They were never best friends or anything like that, but for a year or two the pair of them hung about at lunchtimes, and on the occasional weekend. What connected both of them was their inherently impoverished upbringing; neither Craig nor Dean's family had much money, and so the two would play as part of the same social class. Both of them weren't the smartest kids, and while Dean often received better grades than he did, there was never much between them. While the richer kids travelled outside of school to purchase lunch at the supermarket or at the local café nearby, both Craig and Dean would eat the school lunches together, as they both received it for free due to their upbringings.

One of the moments from Craig's teenage years that he remembers more clearly was when he went over to Dean's house for the first—and the last—time ever. He lived with his mother and father in a council apartment building, but both of his parents were heavy drug users, so he'd often describe his house as more of a crack den than a home. Craig always thought he was being dramatic until he visited it that one time. Needles laying on the ground, empty pill bottles seeped between the carpet, a sty of empty takeout boxes spread across the room—it was a real mess. It made Craig's house look clean, functional and almost idyllic. Even as the they remained upstairs in Dean's bedroom for the majority of his time there, he can still remember Dean's mother's scream as she writhed on the ground, itching for another dopamine intake while his father went out to buy more.

It's not a good memory—not at all—but he does remember it well.

That's why this entire ordeal bothers him. Fifteen years on, and now Dean's living it up in a mansion, while he's not even got a stable roof over his head. And to think the two of them were once equals? Craig feels ashamed of himself.

After an interesting, but mainly backhanded talk about the past and the paths that led them both here, Annie speeds back into the room, panting, a big stupid grin on her face.

"This place is amazing! Please let us stay here, Mr. Dean." She bows down to him and then looks up to her Dad. "Please, Dad. Can you convince him to let us stay here forever?"

CHAPTER SEVENTEEN
Craig & Annie

While he begrudges moving in for a temporary period, he would be blatantly lying if Craig were to say that he didn't enjoy the facade of luxury that he and Annie live in for next few weeks. At first he stayed away from the fancier prospects like the spa or the cinema room, but after a few days of settling in, he enjoyed himself to his heart's content.

Annie, perhaps more subconsciously than physically, begins to feel much better, and resembles the Annie that Craig used to know and love—full of life, full of love and full of a child's energy. When she's not watching the entire *Pixar* catalogue in the cinema room, she's running around the courtyard's lawn, or climbing the jungle gym that's in the back garden. For once, their games of hide & seek are epic and tumultuous; with so many hiding spaces in the mansion, it can take Craig up to two hours to find Annie.

In reality, being unable to find her for two hours actually gives him a bit of a heart attack, but when he *does* find her, it makes everything much better.

Moving into Dean's mansion temporarily wasn't an easy decision, all things considered. It means that Annie isn't going to go to school for upwards of a month or two, which will be a great dent in her education, but if they stayed at the old flat, her mind would be rendered numb anyhow, and so this was the better option.

Besides—she's a smart kid. There's no doubt in his mind that she'll catch up to her classmates sooner rather than later, once she returns.

On sunny afternoons (which are quite the rarity in Scotland), the two spend hours floating around in the pool, enjoying their own company and the security that Dean's mansion has provided them with. It might not quite feel like *home home*, but it does feel like a holiday home. Craig still has to cook, and he's still rubbish at it, but if that's the biggest issue this place has going for it, then that's a good sign.

With all that being said, Craig doesn't get complacent. He doesn't merely sit back and smell the roses—he's still hard at work, contacting agencies and saving up funds from working at the supermarket. With the mansion being a two hour drive from Aberdeen, he's requested that his hours be switched from late at night to very early in the morning, so that he doesn't leave Annie alone in the mansion during the hours where she, and the mansion, would be at its most vulnerable state. Because of this, his hours are cut slightly, but he isn't going to complain.

It's a cruel reminder, but he does ensure to tell Annie almost every night that this isn't going to be their forever home—it's not their home at all, because it's Dean's. They're just guests, and he implores Annie not to forget it. She can enjoy it, but she can't think of it as her own, or trespass the few rules that Dean has laid out for them.

Talking of Dean, he visits the mansion once a week, usually on Fridays, with his two kids, who are a little bit older than Annie. Craig always finds it awkward when Dean visits, like he's a tenant with unpaid rent being visited by his landlord. Dean's kids aren't massive fans of Annie, either; this used to be *their* holiday home. Kids these days don't like sharing, and so when they see Annie sitting on their couch, playing with their gaming console and watching movies in their cinema room, it makes them jealous. Whenever the adults aren't around, they'll call her bad names, like *homeless girl* or *the castle's intruder.* These names hurt Annie and so she doesn't really like either of them much. She doesn't tell Craig about this either, though, as she doesn't want to tattle. If she tattles, then Dean might find out, and then she might be kicked out of the mansion, she fears.

The thing that strikes Craig as awfully unfortunate is the fact that, even after making promises to, that he has not returned to the homeless support group meeting in weeks, even after promising Dorothy, Lines and the rest of them that he would return each and every week. He did message Dorothy to update her on his situation, but a part of him felt exceedingly, and perhaps unreasonably bad about it.

Regardless, it's easy for his mind to wander and forget about the homeless group, and even about his current homeless status, whenever he's indulging in some high-class luxury activities, such as the makeshift mini golf course that Dean had hidden in the cupboard, or tapping his fingers on a grand piano that he doesn't know how to play.

One day, he manages to email his previous landlord through his second email account that he uses only for the most private of emails. Most of the time, he forgets that he even has that account, so it comes as a massive *eureka* moment when he realises that he can do so.

If his landlord just agrees to give his reference to a leasing agency, then there will be no smoke and mirrors the next time that he applies for a property to rent. There would be no obstacles in his way, hopefully, and by the time that he moves out of Dean's mansion, then he should be able to secure a house for his own. By rent, of course, but that's better than nothing—it's a whole lot better than nothing.

"So here's my plan at the moment," he says to Dean one Friday night, "I really appreciate you letting me stay here, I really do, but I need to get out as soon as possible. I don't want to burden you-"

"You're not a burden to me, Craig."

"-Yes, I know, or, well, I guess I didn't *know* that, but my point is that I feel like a burden, whether I am or not. Look, Dean—*this,* all of this, it's great. But it's too great. This isn't me, nor is it Annie. I'm not some successful business tycoon like you are. You've done wonderful for yourself, and you know what? I'm jealous of you."

It is worth noting that Craig has had quite a few beers by this point. His mouth slurs and his eyes flutter open and closed at seemingly random intervals.

"You've done so damn well for yourself, and what have I done? Well, I've screwed my life up, that's what. You've been good to me, but you've been *too* good to me. I don't deserve this—maybe once I fight my way back to the top, I can come visit you again. But I need to leave soon—before next week, and find myself a house to live in. I can't keep leeching off you like this, Dean. We didn't even talk for years until a couple of weeks ago."

"And? What's wrong with a brother helping another out?"

Craig's stomach churls, and he feels sick. "We're not brothers, Dean, not anymore. That was over fifteen years ago. We're completely different people now and we're basically incompatible. If we didn't know each other back then, you wouldn't even take the time to talk to me now. You'd see me for what I am—a man at rock bottom."

"Oh come on now, Craig, you're starting to get on my nerves."

The slightest hint of anger is present in Dean's voice, and it makes Craig stagger. His tongue swirls around in his mouth, hundreds of words ready to be said, but none of them want to be released from his drunken mouth. Be it the truth or not, some things are not supposed to be said, and some things need to stay bottled up inside, at least for a while. Especially when you're drunk, for that matter.

The two make up momentarily, but the glass has been shattered. Dean knows how Craig truly feels and Craig, despite his drunken rambling, will remember what he said and didn't say tonight, and will know that he can't remain in the mansion for much longer.

Annie's not going to be happy, but this entire ordeal is all too false for him. He'd much rather be sat in the homeless group meeting, hearing the grievances of others and wallowing in his own despair, in his own troubles, so that once he rises out of them, he feels accomplished, born anew, with a new chance at life waiting for them both.

That's what Rab would do. He couldn't just aimlessly pass time in his old mate's mansion. He'd get to work, and resolve his issue. Christine was always the same, too—a woman of initiative, she wouldn't just sit down and take Dean's hospitality.

In the final moments of his drunken delirium, just as the light fades from his view and he fades into a deep slumber, he thinks one final, crushing thought.

Maybe Christine should've married Rab instead of him.

CHAPTER EIGHTEEN
Craig & Annie

On Sunday morning at 9AM, Craig packs his few belongings and departs Dean's mansion. Their entire stay lasted about three weeks, which is far longer than Craig was comfortable with. On his way out, he phones Dean, and thanks him for everything that he's done for them and swears to him that he'll make it up to him in the future.

When Craig broke the news of their departure to Annie on Saturday night, he expected more backlash from his daughter, but she surprisingly complied without much of an argument. Perhaps she's felt the same way that he has all this time, or maybe there's something going on behind the scenes that he wasn't aware of—she doesn't seem too bothered to leave, anyhow.

"I'll miss this place," she deadpans, "but I'm happy to go back to Aberdeen. I miss the beach, especially those little rabbits that run about on Beach Boulevard."

Craig wants to say *you're probably not going to see them because we don't live on Beach Boulevard anymore, remember?* But stops himself, realising how utterly crass and rude that would be. Maybe when she gets older, he can whip out the wittier remarks more often.

Returning to the temporary flat, Craig feels a strange sense of belonging. It's not his home — not by any means — but at least here he's in his own family's company. The mould issue should still pose a threat towards Annie, but he hopes that it won't be as much of an emergency due to the cleaning session shortly before leaving for Dean's.

With one single goal in mind, Craig gets straight to work when returning. He inquires into a leasing agency that looks promising, and hones in on a specific property near Kittybrewster that seems both affordable and close to various necessities, like shops, bus stops and a gas pump. There's also a car wash nearby too. *Nice.*

The beacon of hope that really enthused him is his previous landlord's reply to his email, where he reluctantly agreed to provide himself as a reference for any new residence that Craig applies to. He's not sure whether or not the landlord has simply come around and accepted that the fire wasn't his fault, or if he had merely become fed up with him bothering him via all forms of communication. Regardless, both of his references are secured, and things are starting to look not even likely, but definite.

Just before things seem to finalise themselves, though, Craig decides to visit the homeless support group one more time. He doesn't bring Annie with him this time as he sees no reason to. He's not trying to get attention anymore, nor is he as fearful that she'll collapse and pass out in the flat again.

"Hey everyone," he says, after the beginning introductions, "It's good to see you all again. I'm not sure if Dorothy told you, but I was staying with my old friend from school, Dean, and he set me up with a pretty secure place for a few weeks." He omits the part about the *place* being a mansion as he doesn't want to brag.

He continues to relay his current plans, and of how he's saved up enough money to put down the deposit and begin renting a flat. He takes out his mobile and shows the few flats that he's eyeing up, including the one next to the car wash. The group are split between them all, but in the end it's Todd, the elderly man in the wheelchair, that suggests that he go for the residency near the car wash, as it's the cheapest.

Craig couldn't agree any more.

A part of him still feels a little bad, simply showing up to the meeting for the first time in three weeks, just to tell everyone about how he's slowly getting out of his situation, and of how his stint as being homeless is finally nearing its end.

Despite this, no one is bitter. Everyone's congratulatory, and Craig even receives a round of applause after announcing his progression. Lines, who sits next to him just like he did last time, places an affirming hand on his shoulder, essentially saying *told ya so, mate.*

After saying his piece, he enjoys listening to other people's stories. Most of them are positively enthusing, although Zofia's story of how she's still in debt hurts a little. It's mostly good news all around however, which Craig is more than chuffed to hear.

"I'm finally going to be moving into a new flat in a few weeks, people!" Lynda says in jubilation, which sends the room into an uproar of cheers. "My sister's gotten a lot nicer to me now, too, because she knows I'll be gone soon. We're going go-karting with our kids this weekend, you know? We didn't have the money to do that before."

Marwa is the next to share some good news. "Thanks to Dorothy, I got in touch with a refugee support group, and they've helped set me up with a job. I can't thank you enough, Dorothy, but thank you so much. I'm going to be working in a shop."

"I've been saving up a lot more money than I usually do," says Cathleen, "so I'm putting that all into my savings account and I've started to look at houses for rent. It feels so good to be at the stage where you can pick and choose without worrying about prices too much."

Dorothy seems surprised to host a meeting that mostly consists of positive messages and stories, as she's used to poverty and squalor, desperation and suffering. But tonight's meeting gives her hope. It gives everyone hope. It gives them the strength to keep moving forward, towards greater things.

Saying his goodbyes for the night, he well and truly hopes that this would be the last time that he'll see them here. He exchanges numbers with Lines and Elizabeth, as they're the two that he got the closest to, and assures them that he'll keep in touch with them.

Less than a week later, Craig secures a flat viewing of the property in Kittybrewster. It looks even more inviting up close than online, and as he walks through the front door, it already feels like it could be his home. Subconsciously, he maps out the home in his head.

He could put photos of Annie on that mantelpiece, namely the photos taken when she won the egg and spoon race on her school's sports day, or of her and Rab out camping. Fully furnished, there are pieces of furniture littered around, but not quite in the places that he would put them. A big open hall, he imagines pinning up his intercontinental magnet collection, alongside a nice big fancy clock and some hanging decorative flowers, too.

Of course, he no longer has his magnet collection, or a big and fancy clock as it burned down in the fire, but he can get them back. It'll never be the same, of course, but he's certain that he can make it as strong of a home as the old property once was.

He asks about the car wash first and foremost, which gets a laugh out of the landlord, and then proceeds to thoroughly search and scan every nook and cranny of the flat, to ensure that there's no hidden mould or any skeletons in the closet. It's a small flat, but it's a lot bigger than the temporary accommodation that he currently lives in. Positioned on the second floor of a five-story building, the flat consists of a long, winding hallway that connects to four rooms: the toilet, the kitchen and the living room, which is combined but is much larger in space than his current one, and two separate bedrooms.

Two separate bedrooms! Annie will be over the moon when she hears about this.

When the landlord asks him, "how do you like it?", he thinks for a second before he speaks.

"I think it's perfect," he says.

CHAPTER NINETEEN
Craig & Annie

Father and daughter sit side-by-side on Aberdeen beach, staring out at the North Sea. The waves are washing gently, and the sun is shining on this rare bright winters day. There's a small chill in the air, but it isn't strong enough to bother anybody. Seagulls squawk and soar in the air, hunting for the odd chip shop bag that hasn't been snatched up already.

Around three months ago, Craig and Annie sat together on the other side of Beach Boulevard, where they watched their house burn to a crisp, and saw all of their precious belongings disappear forever. It was a devastating night, and it'll probably remain to be the worst night of Craig's life forever—the day that Rab died in the car crash and his house burned down.

Craig hopes for the many, many moments that's left for her in life, that said night is also the worst day of Annie's life, too. He knows that it's somewhat unrealistic to assume so, but as long as she presses through life with pride and courage, then she'll be doing more than enough to make him proud.

Tomorrow, they move into the new flat. It's not a temporary accommodation, nor is it a hostel, or one of Craig's friend's flat—by contract, it is theirs to live in. He didn't want to tell her about it, but he can't hold it in much longer.

Before he breaks the news to her, he glances down at the two printed photographs that he has held in his hand. Because his house burned, he's had to reprint the photos that he had saved of his loved ones on his mobile phone, so they're not the best quality, but that doesn't matter to him. He can still see them, in some way, in some form.

Christine's photo is cropped from their wedding photo. To this day, he hasn't seen a more beautiful woman than Christine that day, in that stunning, regal wedding dress. In that moment, she encompasses all beauty itself—not just the physical kind, but the spiritual kind, too. It was in that moment that he realised that he would never fall in love with any other woman, ever, even if she were to die, which she did.

The other photo, which sees Rab and all of his shiny bald head's allure. In the photo he wears a Scotland football kit and holds a pint of *Tennents'* in his hand, like a true and proper Scotsman. He looks so happy in this photo, but then again he always did. Piss him off one night, and then an hour or two later and that trademark smile would be plastered all over his face again, as if that's just how his face rested. Everyone loved Rab—his funeral was maybe the most busy funeral that Craig had ever attended, and that was *without* many family members, as most of them have perished. The procession hurt, but it also helped heal his broken heart.

Smiling down at his lost loved ones, Craig slides the pictures into his pocket and looks to his side, at the one loved one that's still with him, and perhaps the most important one of all.

"Annie, I need to tell you something." He says.

Her stupid little look is as innocent as ever. He can't help but grin.

"We'll be moving into a new home tomorrow, Annie. Finally, after all this time."

Annie sits upwards, and her lips part to reveal a giant smile. She doesn't say anything, not at first, but simply falls into her father's arms. She doesn't weep, but a single tear falls down her cheek and onto Craig's left arm. Smiling, he rubs her head.

He holds her tight, and she holds him tight. They might have lost everything, but they still have each other, and now they're starting anew under a new roof. They've endured the hardships of homelessness and of all the issues that it causes, both in the short term and in the inevitable long term. But in the present, they're escaping it, and that's a feeling quite like no other. The prospect of a roof over your head, of a bed that's your own, of a warm home to return to on a rainy day. The future is looking bright for them.

Looking out to sea and pointing to nothing in particular, Craig asks Annie, "Tell me, sweetheart, what kind of home would you want to live in?"

Giggling, she says, "There's no houses in the ocean, Dad."

"That's not what I mean. Just look out there and imagine what your dream house would look like. The only rule is that you can't say Dean's house, because that's cheating."

Annie contemplates for a moment, and the longer that she thinks, Craig knows that the answer is going to be more ridiculous. She pats her index finger against her lips, conjuring up the most impossible house interior possible, and Craig knows it.

"I want to live in a house that is made out of diamond and steel, so that no fire or wind can break us down. We'll be super safe, and everyone will love it, too. It'll be on the news."

Craig erupts into laughter. "Well, I think that might be a bit challenging now, but if that's what you want, then I guess I can try and make our home a little bit like that."

"Our home?"

"Yes, Annie. Very soon we'll have something that we can call our own."

ABOUT THE AUTHOR

Hailing from the Highlands of Scotland, Scott G.G Crowden published his debut novel *PARALLAX* on March 20th, 2024. Crowden thrives in creating complex and multi-layered narratives, chock full of interesting, quirky characters and witty humour. He believes that life's issues are most expressively engrossed on a page, and that his writings, while equivocal and open-ended, allow the reader to ponder on the subject topic. Ultimately, his goal when writing is to tackle the hardships of life within the wondrous veil that fiction writing provides for us.

Printed in Great Britain
by Amazon